Once Upon a Time in Chicago

Mary Walsh

Discover other books by Mary Walsh

Once Upon a Time in Chicago

Once Upon a Time in Chicago

Based on actual events

Praise for *Once Upon a Time in Chicago*:

"Mary Walsh takes the reader on a tour of Prohibition/Depression era Chicago as it impacts a struggling Italian family. Executing the perilous balancing act of being true to the facts while producing an interesting narrative, Walsh keeps the reader involved and looking forward to reading more.

As a former Chicagoan who also grew up in a family where foreign accents were common and money came sometimes in buckets, more often in dribbles, Walsh's book took me back to places that only exist in memory today."

- Ray Pace, Best Selling Author of *Disappearing Act*

Chapter 1

South Side, Chicago, 1919

A towering man wearing a dark slate overcoat and a black fedora stepped into the small saloon on West 31st Street on the south side of Chicago. The tavern sat at the junction of the Irish Mob, Little Africa, and Little Italy territories of the city.

Bells on the door jingled and the handful of patrons at the bar turned to see who entered the establishment. Some were laughing and playing cards. Others debated headlines of *The Chicago Daily News*. A din of conversation and a haze of cigarette smoke lingered in the air. The place fell quiet as everyone fixed a concentrated gaze at the stranger. No one dared to move.

The man in the black hat sauntered to the wooden bar, took a seat, silently rested his leather-gloved hands atop the countertop, and waited. As he stared forward, he slowly drummed his fingers on the bar. The other patrons stopped their side conversations.

The owner of the tavern, Bartolomeo Scavuzzo, shuffled in from a back room, wiping his hands on a copiously clean dishcloth hung from his waistband. His wife, Theresa, had ensured that all of his dishcloths were as clean and as dry as could be. He scurried over to the bar, grabbing an empty highball glass. With a trembling hand, he filled it with two fingers full of his best brandy. Without making eye contact, Bartolomeo set the glass in front of the man in the black hat.

"You made me wait," the man in the black hat growled. "I don't like to wait."

"I sorry, Signore Lombardo," Bartolomeo choked nervously, his voice straining. A tightness tingled in his chest. "Won't happen no more." He skittishly motioned to the waiting glass, part of the supply that he had bought from Lombardo. In return for the alcohol, Bartolomeo also had to pay protection money. "*Per favore,* drink."

Lombardo spoke again, "Not good enough. You need fifty more."

Bartolomeo gasped and stumbled a step back. A deep wrinkle formed on his brow. He quickly scanned his livelihood, worried that Lombardo could ruin his business with a simple order to his hired goons. Bartolomeo feared for his life and his family but felt trapped by the call to payment. "*Per favore.* I give you everything I have. *La mia famiglia...* they must eat."

"Figure it out," Lombardo snapped. He rose from his seat, unbuttoned one button on his coat, and pushed it back to present a .38 Smith & Wesson Special strapped to his waist.

A collective gasp echoed throughout the tavern.

"*Si, signore.*" Bartolomeo nodded his head feverishly. He patted his sweaty forehead with a cloth.

"Then we have an understanding," Lombardo hissed. He walked toward the saloon door, leaving the untouched drink on the bar.

"Papa!" Salvatore emerged from the back room, carrying a broom. At 10, he was Bartolomeo's youngest son and he wore corduroy trousers and a newsboy hat. He flung his free hand toward the man in the overcoat. "I heard everything. Why do you let that man speak to you like that?" He jerked his head toward the door in a silent direction for the man to leave.

All noise in the tavern ceased.

Lombardo stopped and glared at the young boy who stood a head shorter than his father. He raised a hand and formed a 'gun' with his thumb and forefinger and pointed it at Sal. As he cocked his pretend gun, Sal stumbled back, knocking over a trash can. Silently, Lombardo faced Bartolomeo once again.

"You need to teach your son to show some respect," Lombardo warned. Ice and fire combatted each other from the tip of his tongue. "If not, he may encounter an..." He glowered at Salvatore once again. "...unfortunate accident."

Lombardo pivoted, opened the tavern door, and walked out. The jingling of the door chimes echoed in the once-again silent tavern. Other patrons had been pretending not to stare at the ominous exchange. Some had quietly exited the tavern, avoiding any possible gunfire.

Bartolomeo exhaled, wiping a wrinkled hand across his sweat-beaded forehead. He didn't want to provoke Lombardo any more than he already had.

"Salvatore!" Bartolomeo scolded his son, now that Lombardo was gone. He didn't want to risk harm to his son. "What you thinking? You cannot speak to Signore Lombardo that way!"

"But Papa, you are a strong man. You taught me to be proud and stand up for myself," Salvatore countered. "I've never seen you act that way, letting someone tell you what to do."

"*Bambino*, some things you learn later," Bartolomeo explained, embarrassed that he cowered in front of his son. He reached for Salvatore and hugged him close.

Out of sight of his regular customers, Bartolomeo snatched the glass of whiskey that Lombardo left behind and dumped it down the drain.

* * * *

Once Upon a Time in Chicago

Bartolomeo and his wife Theresa had six children. The oldest three were born in Sicily: Charlie in 1893, Rose in 1898, and Annie in 1899. After selling the family mule in Sicily for passage money, Bartolomeo left Theresa and the three children for the United States in 1903 in search of the American Dream. He ported in New Orleans and found work in the sugar cane fields. After a year of saving money, he traveled by train and foot up the Mississippi River, calling Chicago his final stop. After Bartolomeo gained stable employment as a laborer, he bought a brick three-flat building on Shields Avenue and a tavern a mile away on West 31st Street.

A year later, Theresa and the children sailed across the Atlantic and registered as immigrants through Ellis Island. They boarded a train and met up with Bartolomeo in Chicago. Over the next few years, three more children were born: Phillip in 1904, Salvatore in 1909, and Faye in 1911. Bartolomeo struggled to learn English in the new land but insisted that his children become fluent and lose the Sicilian accent. Theresa never learned the language of the melting pot nation, instead speaking to her children in Sicilian dialect. She signed English documents with an X.

The family of eight adapted smoothly into the neighborhood full of Italian and Sicilian saloonkeepers, restaurateurs, barbers, and grocers. The neighboring *paesani* formed an exclusive network trying to resist deep prejudice and discrimination from the already-established German and Irish immigrants in Chicago. More immigrants moved to Chicago every week - the Italians, the French, the Chinese, the Russian, and the Greek - each building their own mini-city within the city.

The Sicilians lived in connected homes on narrow streets, sharing a language, clothing style, food, and religion. Santa Maria Incoronata Catholic Church became an epicenter for community activity for them. Many Sicilians didn't leave the neighborhood. They didn't need to, nor did they want to. Women only went to the market, church, or church-related events like baptisms, weddings, and funerals. Men sought camaraderie playing cards with each other in church social halls.

South Side families rooted for the Chicago White Sox a mile away in Comiskey Park, where fellow Italian-American Ping Bodie played. With the Union Stock Yards nearby, a pervading odor of manure, rancid blood, and grease filled the neighborhood air. Peddlers shouted their wares of produce and milk as trolleys clattered down the streets.

As the Italian neighborhood grew, so did crime and the need for protection from it. Giuseppe Lombardo was a bagman for his boss John "Papa Johnny" Torrio. Torrio formed an American Mafia *La Cosa Nostra* racket to sell private security and sold booze to the local Italian business owners. Sometimes, by using his gun, he warned other criminals to stay away from his clients, but often he sent henchmen like Lombardo to collect greenback *pizzo* without providing much safety to the locals. As don of the organization, Torrio became an extremely wealthy and feared man.

If an establishment refused to purchase liquor from the operation, people died.

When Prohibition started on January 17, 1920, taverns either shut down or operated illegally as speakeasies.

In 1925, Torrio decided to retire back home to Italy and gave total control of his $70,000,000 empire of bootlegged booze, gambling, and prostitution to his right-hand man: Al Capone.

Chapter 2

Little Sicily, Chicago, August 1927

Sing a Song of Gangsters
Pockets Full of Dough
Four and Twenty Bottles
Make a Case You Know
-Author Unknown

"Hey, Sal." Paolo jabbed him in the side with an elbow as they sauntered down the sidewalk a few miles from their homes. "You going to college soon, aren't you?" Salvatore and Paolo had gone to high school together at Tilden Tech and became fast friends when Paolo offered Sal his first cigarette. They had studied together, ogled dames, and hung out on each others' stoops watching the world go by.

"Yeah," Sal replied. "My Pops is real proud. All of my older brothers and sisters have gone, so I'm going too. My baby sister Faye will go in a coupla years." He flicked the ash of a cigarette onto the sidewalk and took a drag. A few small groups of people passed them by, rushing to get to the nearby trolley stop. "I'm goin' to the University of Illinois to be a lawyer," he beamed. With the money Bartolomeo had earned from his tavern, he bought rental properties and saved enough money to send his children to college. Getting a higher education was a rare luxury as an immigrant, but Bartolomeo insisted.

"Don't let anyone call you a *lip*." Paolo jabbed Sal in the chest with a finger. "Those attorneys only work for the mob."

"Charlie and Phil would beat me if I ever did that," Sal chuckled, speaking of his older brothers. "And if I'm still alive after that, my Ma will come after me. She might be a head shorter than me and you know she doesn't speak a lick 'a English, but I wouldn't put it past her to put a curse on me."

The friends paraded down North Clark Street in the heart of Little Sicily, Sibley Warehouse on their right. Full of glass windows on the front, the dark six-story building stood adjacent to a small steel bridge crossing the Chicago River. A large sign with white block lettering stating Central Cold Storage Co. indicated the entrance on the ground floor. A few workers stood outside smoking cigarettes on their break. Nearby buildings shot pillars of sooty fumes into the air, giving it a Mephistophelian atmosphere.

Paolo tapped Sal on the shoulder, motioning him to stop.

"Did you hear what happened there?" Paolo asked.

News still spread in Chicago like the Great Fire of 1871. Stories traveled from street vendors to newsboys to trolley drivers to city elite to servants to baristas to clientele and back again.

"What?" Sal questioned.

"Over 1700 cases of government booze was stolen from inside the other night," Paolo explained. "The G. Men went in one morning and it was all gone. Guess President Wilson couldn't make the Eighteenth Amendment stick."

"How do you know all this?" Sal lifted an eyebrow.

"I heard around." Paolo smirked and took a drag of his cigarette.

Sal barked a laugh. "But don't the coppers know that people are still drinking? We're 18 now, so if Prohibition wasn't a law, we'd be able to have a little somethin'. And my Pops would still have his saloon."

"I know," Paolo sighed. "Word on the street is that Bugs Moran's Irish Mob swiped the booze and then Capone's Organization hijacked it from them."

"It's a wonder those two gangs haven't offed each other," Sal said.

Paolo peeked around Sal to make sure no one nearby could hear what he was about to say. He stepped closer to Sal and grabbed the lapel of his shirt.

"I know a place where we can get some hooch," Paolo whispered.

"At a speakeasy?" Sal spoke low. His coal-colored eyes darted up and down the street watching if anyone was paying attention to their conversation. Down the block, a man in a tattered jacket and newsboy cap was selling apples out of a burlap sack, oblivious to their exchange. A truck was revving as it backed up.

"Yeah, my cousin Marco knows a guy who runs one," Paolo stated. "You in?"

"Hmmm...." Sal hesitated and puffed the cigarette dangling in his hand. Sal pondered the consequences of being at an illegal speakeasy. The lure of the carefree lifestyle tempted him away from domestic bliss. If he got caught, he could wind up in the clink. However, the idea of free-flowing whiskey and gorgeous dames appealed to him. "My Pops'll kill me if he ever finds out." Sal pushed his shoulders back and puffed his chest out. The wanderlust intrigued him. "But yeah, I'm in."

"There are lots of women there," Paolo added. "Not girls our age like the ones we knew in school, but *women*. Broads who'll show us things we've never seen before from the girls on the block. Marco told me about how they let you do things to them."

Sal smiled wickedly as the two started walking again. "That'll be aces. I can barely get Lucia to kiss me on the cheek and we've been seeing each other for a few months now."

"Maybe after we go with Marco, you won't need Lucia anymore," Paolo quipped.

"Nah, I like her," Sal said. "She's a sweet gal. And my Ma likes her. If my Ma doesn't approve, then I may as well forget it. My Ma wants me to invite Lucia and her parents over for Sunday dinner." Sal ground the butt of his cigarette into the ground with his shoe.

"Well then, what your Ma and Lucia don't know, won't hurt you," Paolo chuckled. "I'll ask Marco if we can go next week."

"What should I tell my Pops if he asks where I'm going?" Sal begged the question.

"Just tell him I asked you to go to a funeral with me that night," Paolo replied. "Because you'll have to dress up. Somebody's always dyin' around here."

Chapter 3

A week later, Paolo rapped on the front door of the three-story flat on Shields Avenue. The evening sun projected a dark shadow onto the front of the rectangular red brick building. Neighborhood *paesans* lived in similar plain homes along the block. Rich aromas of garlic and onion wafted through the open kitchen windows. Mothers yelled to their bambinos in a mix of Italian and English. A few black lamp posts along the sidewalk flickered on, casting golden halos on the street.

"*Buona sera, Signore* Scavuzzo," Paolo spoke to Bartolomeo as he answered the door. Paolo wore a dark-grey striped three-piece suit with a matching vest, wide lapels, and high-rise cuffed trousers. On his feet, he sported cap-toe oxfords that had been freshly polished. His dark hair slicked back over his head. "Is Sal home?"

Now nearing sixty, Bartolomeo was a short, stout man with a bushy greyed mustache. His silver hair had been slowly receding down his head over the years. He puffed on a half-smoked cigar.

"*Si*, I get Salvatore. You wait here." Bartolomeo directed with his hand. The older man shuffled around and left Paolo waiting alone on the front stoop.

A few moments later, Sal stepped into the doorway where Paolo waited.

"Do I look alright?" Sal motioned to his black trousers that displayed a sharp crease down the front of the wide legs. His pockets were slit on the side and welt on the back with one button closure. He wore a matching loose-fitting jacket and vest. "I had to borrow it from Phil. He has 'bout ten pounds on me but I don't think it fits too bad. What do ya think?"

"That'll work," Paolo replied as he led Sal away from his house. "You ready?"

"Yeah," Sal said. "I told my folks that I'd be gone a few hours to go to the 'funeral' with you." Excitement boiled through him.

* * * *

Fifteen minutes later, the two young men prowled up South Halsted Street, several blocks from Sal's house. Most of the buildings on the avenue had boarded-up windows and solid doors to prevent prying eyes. Paolo and Sal passed frontages displaying flickering signs for a flower shop, a schoolbook store, and a cold storage facility. Small groups of people huddled on the street, smoking. A man in a dark suit, with his hands in his pockets, and a white fedora stood at a boarded-up door, studying passersby on the street.

"I bet that guy is the lookout." Paolo poked Sal in the rib and nodded toward the man waiting by himself.

"Does he let us in?" Sal wanted to know. The nervous anticipation of entering a speakeasy thrilled Sal. He fidgeted as if he could make the secret admittance process go faster.

"Marco said go down the alley and find a dark door with a small red circle on the bottom of it," Paolo replied. "It's near the sewer access. That's how they get the booze in."

The friends came to the end of the block of buildings, quickly edged into the narrow alley, and inched their way along the backside of the cold storage warehouse.

"Do you see the door?" Sal asked Paolo as they searched for the secret entrance, only finding crevices and windows at first.

"It's gotta be here somewhere." Paolo rubbed his hand along the uneven edifice, trying to find any semblance of an ingress. He peered around Sal to make sure no one was around, watching them, and continued his exploration.

"There." As Paolo stood atop a sewer drain lid, he pointed to a dark wooden section of the wall; a small red circle was painted at the bottom near the cement walkway. "This is it." He trailed his fingers along the outline of the door searching for a lever to open it.

Suddenly, a small square section of the top of the door popped open, causing Paolo and Sal to jump back. A man with large ears and a round, hard face peered through the small door. The curve of a grey Homburg hat cast a shadow along his wrinkled forehead.

"Yeah?" the man bellowed through the tiny opening.

"My, um, my..." Paolo stuttered, flustered by the man's abruptness. He took a second to gather himself. "Marco said we could come in."

"You have cash?" the man grunted.

"Yes, in my pocket," Paolo answered. "Ten."

The man shut the tiny door on Paolo's face. Paolo turned to Sal and shrugged. Before he could say something, the man slightly opened the main door, exposing the beginnings of a dimly lit hallway.

Paolo and Sal shuttled inside, careful not to make any sounds, in case an unwanted guest, or a copper, was watching from the outside. Once in the building, the bouncer shut and deadbolted the door behind Paolo and Sal.

"Money," the barrel-chested man instructed. He wore white trousers with a matching vest and tie. A black button-down shirt peeked out beneath his vest. A silver and brown Tommy Gun angled against the wall with its butt on the floor next to him.

Paolo quickly pulled a wad of ones out of his billfold and fanned it.

"Where'd you get all that cash?" Sal talked out of the corner of his mouth.

"Don't worry about it," Paolo whispered.

Before Sal could ask more questions, the bouncer directed them. "Arms out to the sides." Sal and Paolo obliged as the man patted them down searching for guns.

"Good," the large man said. "Follow the rules. No fighting. Or you're kicked out." He cocked his head and nodded toward the hallway for Sal and Paolo to go inside.

"Yes, sir," Sal and Paolo replied in unison.

They walked past the monosyllabic bouncer and wandered down the dark hallway. Jazz music and lively conversation beckoned them at the end. Sal pulled a pack of cigarettes and a lighter from his pocket, plucked one from the package, and lit it up. After he slipped the lighter back in his pocket, he ran his hand along the thick walls that prevented sound from escaping and tipping off authorities. Someone had been thinking when they established the place.

Sal and Paolo entered a large room full of merriment. Sharp-dressed men and women filled the stools in front of the engraved oak bar, a cigarette in one hand and a martini glass in the other. A bartender wearing a white button-down shirt and navy-blue bow tie rattled a shaker full of illegal libations in his hands for waiting patrons. Couples jived on the dance floor to music by

Duke Ellington. Wooden barrels of bootlegged liquor lined the back wall of the room. At a corner booth, a group of men shouted in joy and defeat as they played cards. A pile of cash grew at the center of the table.

A young, attractive woman dressed in a short black fringed and sequined dress that dipped down into a V on her chest approached Sal and Paolo. A yard of pearls wrapped around her neck. "You boys looking for a good time tonight?" she purred as she held a cigarette holder like a wand.

"Yes!" Sal blurted for both of them. The speakeasy was everything he had imagined and more. His nights would be filled coming there.

"Then you came to the right place," she sang.

Sal and Paolo spent the next few hours downing martinis, dancing with dames, and getting accustomed to a new, fabulous lifestyle.

Chapter 4

September 1928

"What do you tell your Pops when we go over to the speakeasy every week?" Paolo questioned Sal as they puffed on cigarettes on Sal's front stoop. "It's not like we have a funeral all the time."

The warm fall air prompted neighbors to come outside on their porches. Children swapped marbles as women batted their rugs into the air.

"Easy," Sal replied. "I tell 'im that I'm meeting a study group at college."

"And your brothers don't suspect nothin'?" Paolo took a long drag of a cigarette.

"Nah," Sal said. "Charlie's busy with his wife and kids and Phil's probably going to his own speakeasy. He's in and out all the time."

"What about your Ma and your sisters?"

"Rose is taking care of her husband, and she's due with another baby soon," Sal explained. "She probably doesn't pay attention to what I'm doing even though they live next door. Faye is helping my Ma around the house. Annie comes around when she can. They're busy."

Paolo chuckled, recognizing they were in the clear.

"How much money did you make last night in that poker game?"

"Twenty-five," Sal answered. "I usually bring home around twenty a week. What about you?"

"Twelve and some change," Paolo moaned. "How'd you win so much?"

"I dunno," Sal chuckled. "Lucky, I guess."

"Yeah, lucky with the ladies, too," Paolo teased. "I counted four different women hanging on you last night. What if Lucia finds out?"

"You mean Sophia," Sal corrected his friend.

"Who's Sophia?" Paolo questioned. "What happened to Lucia?"

"Lucia's old news," Sal sniggered. "I got rid of her when she refused to kiss me. Not like the women we met last night. They were kissing me and putting their hands on me the whole time."

"I saw. So, who's Sophia?" Paolo asked.

"She's my doll on the outside." Sal jerked his head toward the next block full of row homes. An ivory and black Chevrolet Series AB National rumbled down the road in front of them. "She lives down the street. I go out with her when I need to bring a respectable girl if my folks will be there. Like at Santa Maria's. My Ma likes her and has high hopes for us. But I ain't ready to settle down." A group of kids ran by. "I'm having fun. It's not like I can bring one of those broads from the club out in daylight. My Ma would kill me. And then my Pops would drag my body down the street and let the trolley run over it just for fun."

Paolo barked a laugh and playfully jabbed his friend in the chest with an elbow.

"Does your pops ever notice that you've been drinking when you get home?" Paolo asked.

"Maybe," Sal wondered. "He's usually sleeping when I get back. But a few times he's been up listening to the radio. He stares at me but don't say anything. I tell him 'good night' and go to bed."

"How much money you got in your stash?" Paolo talked out of the side of his mouth.

"Almost a grand," Sal said. "We've been playing cards for a year now. It's tucked under my mattress so my Ma don't find it."

"Shit, man," Paolo hissed. "You keep going, you're gonna be like Capone."

"Not even close. I heard his organization brings in five million a week. That's what the paper's said," Sal stated. "But guys at the club said that since the city crime commissioner demanded a ceasefire from Capone in the spring for the upcoming election, things have been quiet for a while."

"That must've been well before Capone's top advisor, Antonio Lombardo, was gunned down during the middle of traffic two weeks ago at the corner of State and Madison by the Aiellos. Capone drilled four of Joe Aiello's brothers in revenge. Marco said it was a bloodbath."

Sal puffed on his cigarette and pondered Paolo's comment. "Do you think we're safe here?"

"Yeah, we're good." Paolo made a sweeping motion with his arms gesturing to the bustling block around them. "We ain't near the heat of it."

"You ever seen Capone?" Sal asked.

"Nah."

"I did."

"Where at?" Paolo asked.

"A few months ago, at my cousin Mary Therese's wedding," Sal said. "Just as she and her new husband were reciting their vows, Capone showed up with a few of his goons. I didn't even know he was invited. The whole church got quiet and watched him walk up to the altar. He planted a kiss on Mary Therese's cheeks, handed her an envelope, and walked out. Just like that."

"Wow," Paolo gasped. "Who in your family knows Capone?"

"I dunno." Sal shrugged. "I have so many cousins I can't keep track of 'em all."

"Did Mary Therese say what was in the envelope?" Paolo wanted to know.

"A hundred bills," Sal answered.

Paolo blew out a low whistle. "Speaking of that, is your pops still paying grease even though he lost his tavern?"

"Nah, I don't think so," Sal answered. "I haven't seen any bagmen come around in a long time. A few years."

"Either your Pops is running something on the inside or he's working with the G. Men," Paolo cackled with a broad smile.

"No way, not my Pops," Sal defended. "He's always been clean. Wants nothing but the best for all of us kids. That's why he always speaks English to us and sent us to college. He was dirt poor in Sicily and doesn't want that life for us. He works hard."

"I'm teasing you," Paolo confessed. "I know your pops and your ma are good people. You have a good place here. Do you think you'll always live in Chicago?"

"Yeah, probably," Sal replied, with a broad smile. "I got dames, I got booze, I got money, my family is here. Why would I wanna go anywhere else?"

Chapter 5

February 14, 1929

"I'm glad you asked me to come with you this morning," Sophia said to Sal. A red wool cap covered her auburn pin curls. She wore a long camel-colored wool coat that covered most of her body. Her gloved hand clasped Sal's elbow as the biting winter wind swirled around them. They wandered down North Clark Street on the north side of Chicago on Valentine's Day.

"Thanks for coming with me," Sal replied. He clutched a large envelope in his other hand. "I need to drop this off and then we can get some brunch."

"I liked having dinner with your parents on Sunday."

"Yeah, my Ma really likes you." Sal almost dropped the envelope.

"Where are we going anyway?" Sophia wanted to know about Sal's delivery.

"I don't know exactly, but my boss said the address is 2116 North Clark Street," Sal said. "He said go inside, ask for Frankie, and give him the envelope by 10:30." Sal checked the watch on his wrist. "It's 10:15 now."

"Do you know what's inside the envelope?" Sophia asked.

"No," Sal answered. "Not allowed. My boss said if I open it then I need to watch my back."

Sophia gave him a side-eye. "Who is this boss of yours? Does he work for Capone or somethin'?" She stopped on the sidewalk next to Sal as if she was unsure she wanted to know the answer to her question. Like most citizens of Chicago, the less she knew about Capone's organization, the better.

Sal ignored her question and gazed up at the row of three-story stores in front of them housing an assortment of ground floor shops: a barbershop, a florist, a cafeteria. Next to the cafeteria was an unadorned concrete building that had a handful of grimy windows.

"I think this is it," he said as he matched the street number of the building to the address on the envelope.

"Sal! Is that you?" a female voice called from down the sidewalk interrupting his thoughts.

Sal and Sophia turned their attention to an attractive blonde woman striding toward them, her ample cleavage peeking out from under her wool coat. A fur stole outlined her neck. "Oh, Sal-ly, it *is* you!" The woman pushed Sophia aside and wrapped her arms around Sal's neck. She planted a kiss on his mouth and smiled, proud of her claimed prize.

"I... Uh... I..." Sal stuttered, frozen in place.

The woman nodded toward Sophia as she slung Sal's arm around her shoulder. "Who's this broad? Ain't I your one and only?"

Sophia wiggled her way between Sal and her new nemesis. "What did you call me?"

"A broad." The blonde woman planted a hand on her curvy hip, challenging Sophia.

Sophia pursed her lips and stared the woman down as if she was about to pull a six-shooter out of a hip holster in the middle of a wild west dirt town.

"Eh," the blonde woman chuckled in Sophia's direction. "You're not worth my time." She turned to Sal and kissed him again. "I'll see you at the club next week, sweetie," she purred. Then she sauntered off down the sidewalk, her hips sashaying in cadence as her heels clicked on the cement.

SMACK!

Sophia's hand slapped against Sal's cheek.

"Who was that... that... floozy?" she shrieked.

"I don't know." Sal rubbed his stinging cheek where Sophia made contact with her leather glove.

"What do you mean you *don't know*?" Sophia screeched. "She obviously knew you!"

"I mean yes, I know her, but I don't know her name," Sal confessed.

SMACK!

Sophia's hand landed across Sal's cheek again.

"What was that for?" Sal gasped, cupping his cheek a second time.

"Even though she's looser than a bag full of change, she still deserves for you to remember her name," Sophia hissed.

"I'm sorry," Sal sputtered. Sal figured that most women wouldn't care about him being respectful enough to remember his side chick's name, but Sophia was classy enough to care.

"Do better next time," Sophia warned.

"Does this mean you forgive me?" Sal spoke softly.

"Not at all," Sophia replied. "Don't speak to me again because we're through!" She huffed, squared her shoulders, and strutted off down the sidewalk.

Sal stood alone on the quiet block, staring at Sophia stride away. A few passersby wandered past him carrying bags and packages from the local shops. "Damn," he muttered. "I screwed that up."

RAT-AT-TAT-TAT-TAT! RAT-AT-TAT-TAT-TAT!

The sound of gunfire consumed the scene. The zip of bullets passed nearby and a puff of dust exploded into the air when one hit an adjoining building.

As his heart thumped in his chest, Sal tried to take cover on the empty sidewalk, huddling down against the nearest building. His chin trembled in fear and he clamped his eyes shut. More shots fired echoing down the block. He wanted to run, but his body froze in fear.

Opening his eyes, Sal scanned the immediate area, placing the source of the gunfire. No one in his line of sight appeared to be hurt or carrying a gun. The others on the street had found safety along the building like he had.

"Is everyone okay?" Sal called from his crouched position trying not to draw attention to himself, unsure if the shooter was still nearby. Gripping the edge of the building, he lifted his head and scanned the surroundings.

A few quiet "yeahs" came from the nearby pedestrians, but no one was brave enough to stand up and try to identify the enemy. Where had the gunfire come from?

After a few silent moments, Sal slowly stood on shaky legs. His hands crumpled the large envelope he had forgotten about. Fearful that a second barrage of bullets would be coming from down the block, and later from his boss if he didn't deliver the envelope, Sal inched along the store frontage and found the entrance to his destination.

Sal snuck inside the door and stepped into an unembellished foyer. A single overhead bare lightbulb provided a lackluster path to an almost empty office area. A stodgy man sat behind a desk, going through a stack of papers.

"Yeah?" the man grunted when noticed Sal.

"Are you Frankie?" Sal asked, glancing side to side, unsure of his surroundings.

"Yeah, who wants to know?" Frankie stood up from the desk, towering over Sal. A holstered gun hung from his hip.

"Me, sir. My name is Sal Scavuzzo."

"That's a funny name... Sal Scavuzzo," Frankie cackled as he chewed on a cigar. "You come right off the boat?"

"No, sir. I was born here," Sal replied. He didn't want to stick around too long but didn't want to anger the large man either by not giving him the answers that he desired.

"Well, whatta ya want, Sal Scavuzzo?" Frankie accentuated Sal's name as if it was a foreign language that could never be translated.

"My boss told me to give you this." Sal held the envelope in front of Frankie and waited in silence for a reaction.

Frankie stuffed his cigar into the side of his mouth, snatched the envelope out of Sal's hand, and ripped it open. As he surveyed the contents, he smiled broadly.

Sal's boss had told him to never open any envelopes that he delivered, but he often wondered what was inside. Money? Photographs? A letter of sale for something? Even though his curiosity wandered, he never gave in. The less he knew, the better.

"Tell your boss that the matter is settled," Frankie stated.

"Yes, sir. I will."

"Now get outta here before I make ya piss your pants," Frankie barked, placing a hand on his holstered gun.

Sal gasped and ran out, Frankie's menacing laughter echoing behind him.

Chapter 6

Late that afternoon, Sal sat inside his parents' kitchen, his nerves still shaking after the day's events. A glass of ice water sweated in front of him on the table. A large cast-iron pot full of his father's sauce simmered on the stove, filling the room with scents of basil, garlic, onion, and oregano. Staring into space, Sal mindlessly drew circles on the table with his finger.

"Salvatore, what you thinking 'bout?" Bartolomeo stepped into the kitchen, interrupting Sal's thoughts.

"Nothin', Pop," Sal sighed.

Bartolomeo walked over to the gas range, lifted the lid on the large pot, and stirred his magical concoction. Another pot sat next to it filled with boiling water, waiting for the pasta to be dropped into it. Without a nod to his son, he said, "Someday I tell you my secret for this."

Sal chuckled. "What do I need to learn to cook for, Pop? I got you and Ma."

"Don't be *idiota*," Bartolomeo warned. He pointed a sauce-covered serving spoon at his small-minded son. "I work hard to send you and your brothers and sisters to college. You lucky. Some *paesans* don't have what you have." With his other arm, he pointed out the new white electric refrigerator on the other side of the room that had replaced a worn-out icebox the previous month.

"I know, Pop," Sal replied.

"When I say you cook, you cook. *Capisce?*" Bartolomeo narrowed his eyes at his youngest son and formed a V between his bushy brows.

Sal stood from the table that was large enough to seat most of his brothers and sisters and assorted nieces and nephews. Ever since Ann, Rose, and Charlie got married and moved out, Sal was thankful for more space in the three-story flat. He used to share a room with Phil, until Phil got married last year and lived nearby with his wife, Joyce. Phil often stopped by the flat where Sal lived with his parents and sister Faye. Even though Phil was married with a baby on the way, he hadn't given up his blithe lifestyle. He often frequented the speakeasies and flirted with the women inside. Sal was on his way to replicating Phil's unbridled behavior.

He strode to his father and hovered over his shoulder as Bartolomeo stirred the thick red sauce. "Can I dip some bread in there?" A set of cast iron skillets hung from the wall above them.

"*Si*. Get new loaf in cupboard," Bartolomeo nodded toward the Hoosier cabinet on the other side of the room. "Your Mama make it this morning. She helping Faye sew. Save some for her."

As Sal stepped away to get the bread, Phil darted into the room clutching the evening edition of *The Chicago Daily News*. He slapped it on the kitchen table, startling his brother and father.

"Did you hear what happened?" Phil exclaimed.

Sal and Bartolomeo stopped what they were doing and rushed over to him.

"Look!" Phil pointed to the thick black headline:

Massacre 7 of Moran Gang

Phil read the secondary line to them, "Assassins pose as policemen; flee in squad car after fusillade; Capone revenge for murder of Antonio Lombardo, officers believe." He pointed to the newspaper text. "It was right on North Clark Street."

"Oh my god," Sal gasped and clamped a hand over his mouth. "I was there this morning. I heard it go down."

"What you doing in North End?" Bartolomeo hissed at his youngest son. "You supposed to be in college. I pay for it." He narrowed his eyes and raised a crooked finger at Sal. "And you lucky your Mama not hear you curse God."

"Sorry, Pop," Sal replied, avoiding his father's question. Recognizing his mistake that he didn't think before he spoke, he should have told his Pop that he was with Sophia.

Sal's father didn't need to know that he had been doing side jobs for Eddie Devine, a law associate of Al Capone. He was paid $40 a week as long as he didn't ask questions about envelopes he delivered or packages he received for Eddie. If his job took him to the far end of the city and out of class, the money was worth it.

Phil glared at his brother, caught on to the guise, and changed the subject back to the newspaper. "Word is out that four men entered a garage on North Clark and two of them were dressed as cops, but nobody's talking. Nobody knows who did it."

"Oh, come on," Sal balked. "Everyone knows who did it."

"I'm just saying--" Phil answered.

"Enough," Bartolomeo interrupted, leaning between his sons. "We safe and we *famiglia*." He walked back to the range, dipped his spoon into the pot of sauce, and tasted it. "Mmm. Almost done." He dropped several large handfuls of homemade linguini into the boiling water of the second pot.

Once Phil realized his father wasn't paying attention, he whispered to Sal, "What are you getting into? Why were you on North Clark this morning? That's a good ten miles away from here."

"I was with Sophia," Sal answered. "I swear. You can ask her. Well, maybe not..."

"Why not?" Phil balked.

"She broke up with me this morning." Sal glanced at Bartolomeo inhaling the aroma of his special sauce. "Don't tell Pop yet. I'll tell him when I'm good and ready."

"Okay," Phil said, eyeing his brother suspiciously. "As long as you're not doing somethin' stupid."

"What about you?" Sal hissed. "You're out every night with a different girl. What does Joyce say about that? I see your fancy clothes and the wads of cash. I know what you're doing. I'm not dumb. Or, as Pop likes to say, *idiota*. Look at you. You got those pants at Marshall Field's." Sal pointed. Marshall Field's was one of the largest department stores in the world, catering to upscale clientele with leather shoes, fine suits, and mink coats. "How can you afford them?"

Phil wore a white button-down shirt, a thin black tie, and brown checkered woven trousers. Even though he was five years older, he stood eye to eye with Sal. The brothers could have passed for twins with their heads of coal-black hair and dark bushy eyebrows.

"How do you know how much my pants cost?" Phil argued.

Sal shut his mouth. His big brother had him. Sal owned a pair of similar trousers that he bought at the largest department store in the city and wore to the club every week--along with a pair of brown and white leather oxfords he found in the shoe department.

"I thought so." Phil huffed in victory. A bemused smile spread across his face.

Sal's cheeks burned.

Bartolomeo interrupted them from across the room, "Call your Mama and your sisters. Pasta is ready."

Chapter 7

"Can you pass the bread?" Sal spoke as he and his family gathered at the kitchen table eating Bartolomeo's pasta. A large salad sat in the center of the table next to the pot of sauce-covered linguini. "I never got a chance to dip some earlier."

His older sister Annie sat to his left. She left her children with her husband for a visit and handed Sal a plate of crusty Sicilian bread, freshly made by Theresa that morning.

Sal snatched it from her and put three pieces on his plate.

"Hey! Save some for the rest of us!" Annie reprimanded him.

"You had the last piece," Sal retorted. "I pulled open the cupboard the other night and it was all gone."

"I did not!" Annie shot back. "I wasn't even here."

"No, she didn't," Phil interrupted. "I did."

Sal turned his attention to his brother. "You!" He poked Phil with a fork in the shoulder.

"Enough!" Bartolomeo interrupted them. "You act like *bambini*! Quiet now. I want to eat in peace."

"*Perché stai combattendo?*" Theresa spoke about her squabbling children. She had been quietly listening to her family argue. Even though she didn't speak English, her deep-set eyes spoke volumes to her children. Time had made its mark on her hardened face.

"Look what you did," Faye admonished her older brothers and sister. "You're upsetting Ma. We're not fighting, Ma." With her fork, Faye swirled a small mound of pasta on her plate.

"Sorry, Mama," Sal lowered his voice. "We don't mean to fight in front of you."

"Speaking of fighting," Annie said, "did you see the paper this afternoon?"

"Yeah," Sal and Phil replied in unison.

"They're calling it the St. Valentine's Day Massacre," Annie expressed, as she swallowed a bite of pasta. "Remember when Antonio Lombardo was gunned down in September? That's what they're saying this was for."

"Lombardo?" Sal questioned. "Why do I know that name? Not just from September and today, but I've heard it before."

"Antonio Lombardo worked for Capone, that's why," Phil answered as he shoved a heaping forkful of pasta into his mouth.

"Nah, that's not it," Sal mused. "I feel like I met someone with that name."

Crash!

Bartolomeo dropped his fork onto the edge of his plate and made a clattering sound. Everyone faced him in surprise.

"*Bastardo*!" Bartolomeo bellowed and flung his fingers into the air. "Curse him!"

"Pop, did you know Antonio Lombardo?" Faye wanted to know. She set her fork down on the table in anticipation of her father's reply.

"Not him," Bartolomeo replied. "His cousin Giuseppe Lombardo. He bomb my tavern."

"What?!" his children shrieked together.

"What are you talking about, Pop?" Phil eyed his father. "Your tavern was bombed? You never told us it was bombed."

"Because of you, Salvatore." Bartolomeo poked a bent finger at his youngest son.

"Me? Why me?" Sal pointed his fork toward himself.

"When you *bambino*," Bartolomeo began, "Giuseppe Lombardo collect money for La Cosa Nostra. You disrespect him."

Sal gasped. "I remember that. I was ten years old. I was helping you clean the tavern that day."

Bartolomeo continued, "He said if I don't teach you behave..." Bartolomeo's voice trailed off as if he imagined the worst for his son.

"That something would happen to me," Sal finished his father's sentence with a shudder. "I remember that."

"*Si*." Bartolomeo nodded. "You right, Salvatore, when you told me I cannot let him speak to me *minacciosamente*."

"*Minacciosamente?*" Faye wondered out loud.

"Threateningly," Phil translated. He let their father continue the story.

"I not pay him next time," Bartolomeo explained. "And he bomb my tavern." Bartolomeo slammed a fist into the table, clattering the water glasses.

"How did we not know this?" Sal wanted to know.

"You *bambino*," Bartolomeo replied. "You not understand." He wiped his furrowed brow with a cloth napkin. "I put all money into tavern. I have to start all over again and buy buildings to send you to college."

"It's okay, Pop," Phil said, motioning to the well-equipped kitchen around them. "We are fine now. We have everything we need and then some. Your properties provide plenty for us."

Annie lowered her head as she spoke, "Were you hurt, Pop? When he bombed the tavern?"

"No," Bartolomeo said. "Tavern on fire. We here." He held Theresa's hand in his, thankful that he kept his family safe.

"*Il mio amore*," Theresa spoke to her husband.

"*Ti amo*," Bartolomeo said back to her. Lovingly, he stroked a finger along her cheek and kissed her.

"Why didn't you tell us this, Pop?" Phil questioned. "Me and Charlie could have done something."

"I protect you." Bartolomeo stood from the table and made a sweeping motion with his arm. "All of you. The less you know, you keep safe."

"I guess it makes sense now," Sal put it all together. "That happened in 1919 and Prohibition started the following year. Pop would have had to close the tavern anyway. No wonder we hadn't heard much about it."

"That's true," Phil concurred.

Bartolomeo settled at his place again at the head of the table.

The family chatted the rest of the way through dinner, as they did every night.

Chapter 8

September 20, 1930

"Hey, Paolo," Sal said, "you see that woman over there? Do you know her name?" He and Paolo settled in at the end of the bar at the speakeasy. Through the crowd, Sal pointed to the voluptuous blonde woman. Her short flapper dress hugged every curve. A long strand of pearls wrapped twice around her neck. She wore a black fur felt cloche hat that shaded most of her face. Her lips were lined in ruby red.

"Yeah, that's Mae Russo. She's a real looker."

Other men in the room gawked as Mae plucked a mirror and lipstick from a small purse and applied a fresh stain. Women nearby rolled their eyes at her obvious ploy to attract a man.

"Yeah, she is. I haven't seen her in a while. I couldn't remember her name," Sal replied. "She's the reason that Sophia broke up with me last year."

"Really?" Paolo exclaimed.

"I remember that me and Sophia were up on North Clark and Mae came walking down the sidewalk and kissed me in front of Sophia. Then Sophia slapped me across the face. Twice." Sal rubbed his chin recalling the sting.

"Twice?"

"Yeah, once for Mae kissing me and then again because I didn't know Mae's name."

Paolo chuckled at his friend. "Sophia's a classy broad so I guess she was just looking out for other broads." Paolo laughed again. "You sure screwed that up. She was your good dame on the outside."

"Don't I know it," Sal lamented. "My Ma and Pop were pretty mad at me then. But she's old news. I have lots of women here to talk to."

The friends gawked as Mae strutted in their direction.

"Seems like Mae is interested in you again," Paolo told Sal.

Mae caught Sal's gaze and weaved her way through the crowd that separated them.

As she approached them, Mae held up an unlit cigarette in her gloved hands. "Hi again, Sal. Got a light?" she asked, measuring him up.

"Yes... yes..." Sal stuttered as he fumbled for a lighter in his pocket. He couldn't take his eyes off of Mae. She was several years older than Sal and Paolo.

Sal pulled out a lighter and flicked it a few times close to Mae's cigarette. Once her cigarette was lit, she sucked on it and blew a thin cloud of smoke into the air. Paolo took note of Mae's interest in Sal and stepped away to flirt with other women.

"I haven't seen you in a good year," Sal said. "Where've ya been?"

"Around." Mae changed the subject, "Aren't you asking me what I want to drink?"

"Yes, of course," Sal said, entranced with the idea of enticing an experienced older woman. "What do you want to drink?"

"An Old Fashioned would be nice," Mae purred as she closed the gap between them.

With a finger wave, he caught the attention of the barkeep. "Two Old Fashioneds, please."

The bartender mulled a sugar, bitters, and water concoction. Then he added ice and two-fingers of whiskey to the glasses.

"That'll be two dollars, please," the barkeep said to Sal.

Sal reached into his billfold and laid a Lincoln on the bar. "Keep the change." He grabbed the drinks and handed one to Mae.

"Wow, you're a big spender." Mae crushed her cigarette into a nearby ashtray. "I oughtta stick with you for a while." She caressed his forearm.

"Yeah, stick with me and I'll show you a good time," Sal boasted, feeling the power of a promise of future intimacy with her. He'd be a real man then. He slipped an arm around Mae's tiny waist.

Mae replied, "I bet you would."

"Do you wanna dance?" Sal asked, discovering tiny flecks in her eyes. He couldn't wait to discover more about her.

"I thought you'd never ask," Mae answered. The whole room seemed to quiet to soft murmur when she talked.

They downed their drinks, Sal grabbed Mae's hand and led her to the dance floor. He pulled her close as they danced to *Let's Misbehave*. Other couples surrounded them in the center of the large, lively room.

"Who taught you how to dance?" Mae asked breathlessly, her bosom lightly heaving up and down.

"My two older sisters," Sal replied as he twirled Mae around and then dipped her.

"They taught you well," Mae said. "What else do you know how to do?"

Sal chuckled at Mae's flirting. "I know a lot of things," he said.

"Besides kissing?" Mae winked at him. "It's been a year since you kissed me. You haven't lost your touch, have you?"

"Only one way to find out," Sal bantered back. Even though he had kissed Mae before, and caused Sophia to slap him, this was the first time he imagined whisking her away to a private place to discover what lay beneath her dress. He became so focused on the sensation of Mae's body next to his that he forgot where they were.

With one hand behind Mae's back in the dip, Sal trickled his fingertips along Mae's shoulders toward her collarbone. Mae giggled in response. He stared into her blue eyes and boldly kissed her freshly-stained mouth. He held her there for a good minute as the crowd around them seemed to hush.

Once Mae came up for air, she had to catch her breath. "Wow. You weren't kidding that you know a lot of things."

Sal lifted Mae upright and held her close to him. A floral aroma lingered in her hair. He couldn't wait to entangle his limbs with hers. His heart pounded in his chest.

"If you wanna get out of here, I can show you more," Sal whispered in her ear. The idea of bedding an older, gorgeous woman flushed all common sense out of his mind.

Mae smiled broadly. "I'd love to take you up on that offer, but I can't tonight."

"You have other plans?" Sal questioned. He assumed other suitors were interested in Mae. She was attractive and charming. Her curves could stop a man cold.

"Yes," Mae answered. "I need to leave in an hour."

Sal wondered about Mae's mysterious plans. If things progressed with Mae as he hoped, he didn't want to share her. At least not here at the speakeasy.

For the next hour, Sal danced, laughed, drank, and flirted with Mae.

As they lingered at the exit door, Mae leaned into Sal and kissed him on the mouth. "I loved spending time with you, Sal-ly. I hope we can do it again."

"How about next Saturday?" he offered, loosening his tie. "Here. At 8:00. We can dance and drink a while and then maybe spend time on our own. What do ya say to that?"

"I'll be there with bells on." Mae smiled wide and winked at Sal.

Chapter 9

A few days later, Sal and Paolo ate breakfast at the counter of Lou Mitchell's diner, a mile north of Little Italy on Jackson Boulevard. Other patrons filled the establishment, which boasted serving the world's finest coffee in red neon script letters on the outside of the building. The aroma of bacon and coffee filled the air.

"You going to the card game tonight?" Paolo asked Sal as he cut up his omelets.

"Yeah, I gotta do something for my Pop before I head over," Sal replied.

"What's he got you doing?"

"He ordered a new electric washing machine when he first learned about them a few months ago and it finally came. He needs me to help him put it together." Sal scooped a spoonful of scrambled eggs onto his fork and took a bite.

"How long do you think it'll take?" Paolo asked.

"An hour maybe." Sal shrugged. "Hopefully the thing came with instructions. Then I gotta do some studying."

"Well, I'm gonna head over around seven..." Paolo said.

"I should be there by nine," Sal finished his friend's sentence.

"What's going on with you and Mae now?" Paolo wanted to know. "I saw you kissing her the other night."

"Hopefully something," Sal replied. "We made plans to meet up again on Saturday."

"You think you could take her around your Ma and Pop?" Paolo broke his bacon in half and stuffed it in his mouth.

"Nah," Sal said. "She's not a classy broad. You know my Pop likes it quiet. And my Ma would hate the way Mae dresses. She might curse at me in words I don't know."

Paolo laughed out loud.

The friends finished eating their breakfast and a matronly waitress slapped a receipt on the lacquer counter. "That'll be a dolla five, fellas." Her auburn and silver hair was bound into a tight twist at the back of her head. Her name was stitched on the left breast of her white uniform dress. A matching apron with multiple pockets surrounded her ample hips.

"Thanks, Thea." Sal pulled a dollar out of his billfold. Paolo did the same and the friends shared a side glance about their favorite waitress. "Keep the change." Even though Thea never had children of her own, they loved her like a second mother.

"You two are my best customers," Thea beamed. "See you next week."

"I gotta go." Sal stood. "Gotta study for an exam before I go out tonight."

* * * *

At 9:15 that night, Sal rushed into the back room of the speakeasy, out of breath. He found an empty seat at the large round table opposite Paolo. A thick haze of cigar smoke filled the dark room. A bare bulb hanging from the ceiling provided the only light in the room. Burning ash from lit cigars produced glowing red circles, giving the room a nefarious atmosphere.

"Glad you could join us, Sal," the large man to his right grunted. A large mound of multicolor plastic chips filled the space in front of him. "You can come in the next round."

"How much you bring tonight?" the thin man to his left asked him. He sucked on a glass full of hooch.

"Enough," Sal replied. He pulled a wad of bills out of his pocket and laid it on the table. Earlier that night, after he had helped his Pop install the new washing machine, he grabbed all of his winnings from under his mattress. He had been on a winning streak lately and hoped to double his pot.

The man on his left blew out a low whistle. "If I didn't know any better, I'd think you were working for Capone."

The regulars at the table whooped in laughter. The various-sized men puffed on half-gone cigars and swallowed glasses of whiskey.

"Maybe. Maybe not," Sal countered. He snickered knowing the word on the street that most of the men at the table probably did some kind of business for Al Capone's organization. If they didn't, they wouldn't be sitting there.

The other players finished the round and Sal exchanged his cash for some chips. The man next to Paolo dealt the next round.

"Ante up," the dealer directed. Each of the men at the table tossed a couple of chips into the middle of the table to build the pile. "A dollar you put on the button goes to the house."

Sal peeled his five cards from the table and snuck a peek at his hand. Hoping not to give away his elation, he smiled slightly at an ace of spades and an ace of diamonds. The other cards consisted of a five of hearts, a seven of hearts, and a ten of clubs. A pair. Not a bad start. He decided to hold onto the aces and the ten, just because it was the high card of the remaining three.

Players traded the bad cards in hopes of better ones. When it was Sal's turn, he laid down the five and the seven. "Two for me."

The dealer next to Paolo slid two new cards across the table to Sal. He picked them up and tried to hide his excitement at an ace of hearts and a ten of diamonds. Full house. Only three other combinations of cards could beat his hand. He felt pretty good as he lit up a cigarette.

The others around the table bid on their hands. Sal was excited that he was invited to play with an established group. The rare invitation set off a confident spark inside him.

"Five."

"See your five and raise you two more."

"Ten."

Sal matched each increase and silently waited for the pot to grow. The more he stayed quiet, the better chance he had to walk away with all the money.

"I see your ten and raise you five more."

Paolo huffed and contemplated his hand. "That's too rich for my blood. I'm out." He laid his cards down on the table and pushed his chair back as he waited for the others.

When it was Sal's turn, he glanced around at his competition. The large man to his right had already folded. The thin man on his left was still in but wiped a bead of sweat from his brow. Sal was confident that he had a better hand. The dealer was still in, but Sal couldn't read him. Maybe he was bluffing. The pile of chips in the middle of the table was close to seventy dollars. A small grin formed on the corner of Sal's mouth. He was confident he would win among these arrogant men.

The dealer studied his cards then threw a handful of chips on the table. "Twenty-five."

The thin man next to Sal swallowed hard. "I gotta fold." He laid his cards down on the table in defeat.

Sal matched the twenty-five.

"Just you and me, Sal," the dealer hissed.

Thawing ice in a drink clattered, making the only sound in the room. The other men at the table glared in silence, waiting for Sal's answer. He was the David to the dealer's Goliath and hoped for the same result.

"I'm still in." Sal refused to fall to the pressure and studied the man figuring out his tell. But nothing showed. With his right hand, Sal fluttered the tops of the cards in his left hand in an attempt to intimidate his competitor.

"Sicily Boy, this is a man's game." The dealer stared Sal down and pushed his entire pile of extra chips into the center of the table. He snickered to the other players as if he had already won.

"Well, that's fine, because I'm a man," Sal countered and shoved his pile of chips into the growing mound of money. He had something to prove against the haughty man. Sal was confident that his full house was enough to take the pot home.

"Call," the dealer said. He laid his cards down one at a time face up. He had a five, six, seven, eight, and nine. Of spades.

Sal's mouth fell open. The sparks in his brain desperately tried to connect what just happened but instead caused a short circuit. Sal deeply rubbed his face with both hands comprehending everything.

The dealer's straight flush beat Sal's full house. He lost all of his hard-earned money. In the first hand. Gone. What an arrogant fool he was.

"I told you this was a man's game," the dealer sniggered. With a heavy arm, he shoveled the entire mound of chips toward himself. He glared at Sal with narrowed eyes, taunting him to try and beat him again.

Sal sank into his chair in defeat. He had nothing left in his pockets to bet. He couldn't stay at the table and watch the rest of the men play poker. Nor did he want to go home.

Paolo picked up on his friend's embarrassment. "Come on, Sal, I'll buy you a drink. I need a break."

Chapter 10

A few minutes later, Sal and Paolo settled onto the wooden chairs that surrounded the lacquered bar. The room was full of drinkers, dancers, and conversationalists. Laughter and music filled the air. Scantily clad women traversed the floor holding trays of fresh cigarette cartons for sale.

"I can't believe I lost all my dough." Sal trounced his sorrows with a glass of bourbon. "Everything's gone. I got squat!"

"Don't worry," Paolo consoled him. "You'll make it back. You always land on your feet."

"But what if I don't? I'm supposed to meet Mae here on Saturday. She'll want me to buy her a few drinks, I'm sure." He lowered his head in shame. "She's a play girl. She expects the best. I need to show her a good time."

Paolo slapped a hand on Sal's shoulder. "How about your job with Eddie?"

"Eh, he calls for me when he needs me. Usually every week. But I haven't heard from him yet. I don't have time to wait for him. I need the dough now."

Paolo glanced around the room making sure no one could hear what he was about to say. "I wish I could help you, but I'm scraping by as it is. If you want, my cousin Marco knows a guy."

"Oh yeah?" Sal's face perked up. "Funny I've never met your cousin, but he always knows how to hook us up."

"Shh. Shh. We gotta lay low about this. I don't want word getting out."

"Sure, sure," Sal replied. "Whatever you say." He inched closer to Paolo so that no one could hear their conversation. "What's the low down?"

"Marco has a guy who can lend you some money," Paolo whispered. "He's a butter and egg man."

"Okay," Sal replied. "I'm on board."

"Are you out of your mind? You can't just say that," Paolo warned. "When he lends money, you have to pay interest back to him."

Sal leered at his friend. "How much?"

"Fifty."

"Fifty dollars?" Sal scoffed. "I can make that in a week."

"No, fifty percent," Paolo corrected him. "If he loans you three hundred, you pay him four-fifty."

"Oh." Sal sighed.

"And if you don't pay him back within two weeks," Paolo warned, "he sends his guys to fit you for cement shoes and they toss you in Lake Michigan. He don't fool around."

Sal swallowed hard.

"That's why we gotta lay low about it," Paolo added.

Sal pondered the proposition while he swallowed the bourbon. If he borrowed the money, he could buy drinks for Mae on Saturday, play more poker, and he'd have enough to last until his next job with Eddie. It all depended on what Eddie had for him. Sal wasn't sure why Eddie hadn't contacted him yet this week. That was unlike him. If he only borrowed fifty, he could easily pay back seventy-five in two weeks. As long as Eddie had a job for him.

"I'm in," Sal said.

"You sure?" Paolo responded. "I don't want you getting into something you can't handle. You're my *goombah*. I don't want you taken for a ride. *Capisce?*"

"Yeah, I'm sure," Sal replied.

* * * *

The next afternoon, Sal stood with Paolo up the block from his three-story flat on Shields Avenue. They puffed on cigarettes to keep warm in the unexpected September chill. A street peddler bundled in a winter jacket strolled by selling peanuts out of his cart. Paolo waited for the man to be out of earshot before he spoke.

"I talked to Marco," Paolo whispered. "He said to go to Bella Napoli Cafe on South Halsted Street at 2:00 tomorrow."

"That's near the speakeasy," Sal deduced.

"Yeah," Paolo replied. "You'll meet the Big Shot, Joe Aiello, in the back corner booth."

"Joe Aiello the gangster?"

"Yeah, him."

"What's he want with a nobody like me?"

"I dunno. Maybe he owed Marco a favor from way back?" Paolo shrugged. "But he agreed to meet you."

Sal pondered the notion as he took off his hat and studied the brim.

"Just one more thing," Paolo directed.

"What's that?"

"Wear your Sunday best," Paolo said. "He don't like bums. If he approves you, he'll lend you the dough."

"Okay, thanks," Sal replied. "I owe you."

"Fuhgeddaboudit." Paolo smiled broadly at his friend.

Chapter 11

At 1:50 the next afternoon, Sal hustled down South Halsted Street. A block away, a trolley clanged its bell. Dozens of peddlers in their horse-drawn carts filled the edges of the wide avenue. Locals were out buying groceries and provisions.

Wrapped up in a long overcoat that fell to his knees, a fedora on his head, and black gloves, Sal pushed himself against the crowd. He couldn't be late--not if he wanted to make a good impression on Joe Aiello.

In the past six hours, Sal asked around about the Big Shot. He was a bootlegger and organized crime leader in Little Italy. He ranked seventh on the Chicago Crime Commission's list of Public Enemies. Aiello coordinated machine gun ambushes and masterminded hits. Even though he was also Italian, and not Irish like his ally Bugs Moran, he had a long-standing feud with Al Capone.

Why Aiello agreed to meet with a nobody like Sal, he couldn't comprehend.

Sal approached Bella Napoli Cafe, its entrance veiled by a massive red and white striped dome awning. On the side of the awning, a large white banner displayed **Special! Italian Dinners 55¢ & 80¢** in big block letters.

With nerves kicking in, Sal entered the eatery. His stomach knotted up and his palms moistened with sweat inside his gloves. His heart thumped against his ribcage, jerking his pulse. As Paolo had directed, Sal wore his Sunday best: a blue pin-stripe suit with a matching tie. If he didn't say everything right to Joe Aiello, he could easily be taking his last few breaths.

As Sal wound his way around several four-seater bistro tables filled with patrons, he spotted a clean-shaven man with dark hair sitting in the back corner booth. Two of the man's swarthy, emotionless associates stood nearby, guarding the vicinity. Sal spotted a pair of six-shooters strapped to each man's hip and briefly looked away so as not to disclose his nerves.

"Mr. Aiello?" Sal spoke softly to the seated man who appeared to be in his late 30s. "I'm Sal Scavuzzo."

"You're early, kid," Aiello said. He wore a dark grey three-piece suit with a black and white patterned tie. "I like you already." The previously stoic henchmen laughed at their boss's simple joke.

Sal smiled weakly, trying hard to not show his fear of the intimidating man.

"Have a seat." Aiello motioned across from him to the empty side of the booth.

Sal scooted quickly into the booth and sat upright.

"How old are ya, kid?" Aiello asked.

"I just turned 21, sir," Sal answered. His nerves slightly lessened knowing that he got that question correct.

"I hear you want me to help you out," Aiello spoke again. He pulled a toothpick out of the table dispenser and put it in the corner of his mouth. "It's gonna cost you."

"Yessir. I... I'd... like to borrow some money," Sal uttered. He inhaled a deep breath and waited for a response.

Aiello smiled wide, a toothy grin spread across his face, the toothpick dangling out of his mouth. "You expect *me* to lend you money?"

"Yes... sir," Sal stuttered. He nervously wrung his hands together on his lap beneath the table.

"You're honest," Aiello said. "I like that."

Again, his goons laughed.

"How much?" Aiello asked.

"Fifty dollars, sir," Sal spoke just above a whisper. Sal needed more than fifty but didn't want to get in too deep with Joe Aiello. As long as he found work in the next two weeks, he could easily pay the money back plus fifty percent.

"I heard on the street you work for Eddie Devine, don'tcha?" Aiello changed the subject.

"Yes, sir. I do," Sal answered. He wondered what his boss had to do with borrowing money.

"And he's a Capone *lip*?" Aiello inquired. Sal guessed that Aiello already knew the answer.

"Yes, sir. He's an attorney for Mr. Capone," Sal said. "Though I've never seen the two of them together."

A sly grin formed out of the corner of Aiello's mouth. "Tell ya what," he said, "I'll loan you the money if you do something for me."

"Anything," Sal answered. He breathed a small sigh of relief that this conversation was going better than he expected.

"Normally, I don't lend out Grant's chump change," Aiello explained, "but what you can do for me is worth much more."

Sal listened quietly and sat motionless. He had no idea what he could offer Aiello. The mob boss had everything he could want.

A passing waiter dressed in a white tuxedo shirt and black slacks caught Aiello's eye.

"Hey, Jimmy," Aiello called to the lithe server. "Get me some minestrone."

Jimmy approached the booth in two steps. A white cloth napkin was draped over his wrist. "Yes, sir, Mr. Aiello."

Aiello temporarily turned his attention on Sal. "Kid, you want some minestrone?" Sal didn't have a chance to answer before Aiello spoke again. "I get you some. It's the best in Chicago."

Sal nodded his head in accepting the offer even though he felt like his answer didn't matter to the crime boss.

"Two bowls of minestrone," Aiello said to Jimmy.

"Yes, sir, Mr. Aiello," Jimmy answered. "I'll bring it right out." And he scurried off.

Aiello focused on Sal again and pulled his billfold out of the inside breast pocket of his gray suit. He opened it up and laid a crisp fifty-dollar bill on the table between him and Sal. "That's yours, kid, if you do something for me."

"Anything," Sal repeated. He quietly gulped at his words knowing they might be the last of him but willed himself to believe that everything would be okay. His date with Mae was worth it.

With two fingers, Aiello slid the money across the table to Sal. "I need to know where Capone is. And, you, my young friend, will find out for me."

Sal wanted to object because he had no idea how to track Aiello's biggest rival, but he knew if he did object, Aiello might do something worse to him than not lend him the money.

Aiello stared Sal in the eyes and spoke again, "I know you'll do this for me."

"Yes, sir," Sal whispered. He couldn't refuse Joe Aiello. Not if he wanted to avoid a trip in the meat wagon.

Aiello reached into his pocket again, pulled out a small business card, and handed it to Sal. The card read "Chicago Sugar Supply Co." and listed SOU-8833 as the telephone number. Sal didn't recognize the company and guessed it was a fake name to cover illegal activities.

"Get on the horn and call this number when you know something," Aiello directed.

"Yes, sir," Sal repeated, as he quickly shoved the money and card into his breast pocket.

"You have two weeks to pay me back the money," Aiello instructed. "$75."

"Do I also call you when I have it?" Sal asked.

"No," Aiello replied. "I'll find you. *Capisce*?"

"Yes, sir."

"I knew you were a good kid," Aiello joked. He reached across the table and slapped Sal across the cheek. Aiello's hatchet men laughed again.

Jimmy came by with two steaming bowls of minestrone and Sal feasted like it was his last meal.

Chapter 12

On the following Saturday night at 8:00, Sal sashayed into the speakeasy to meet Mae. He wore a white button-down shirt with a blue vest and matching trousers. His coal-black hair was slicked back. He found Mae chatting with a group of men at the end of the bar. She was smoking a cigarette. A half-full glass of amber liquid rested on the counter in front of her. Sal's mouth watered at her deep-cut dress that showed off her ample bosom.

He pushed his way through the men and stood next to Mae.

"Hi-ya, Sal-ly," Mae said with a curl of her lips. She flipped her blonde hair back and crossed her legs. "You look snazzy tonight."

"Hi, Mae," Sal replied. "How are ya?' He nodded toward her glass. "What're you drinking?"

"Hooch," she answered. "Neat." Mae took a long drag of her cigarette and slowly blew the smoke into Sal's face as an invitation to spend the night with her.

Sal nodded toward the barkeep. "Can I get your best hooch? Neat."

The man nodded and grabbed a glass on a nearby shelf and filled it with the auburn libation. He slid it in front of Sal. "One dollar."

Sal reached into his vest pocket and pulled out the fifty that Joe Aiello lent him and laid it on the bar. "Sorry, that's all I have."

The bartender grasped the money and stepped away to get change.

Mae noticed the large bill and snickered. "Another big spender night, huh, Sal-ly?" She crushed her cigarette in a nearby ashtray.

"Only the best for you, Mae." Sal winked at her. He slid an arm around her tiny waist and pulled her close. The space between them was only separated by their clothing.

Mae gasped in response and slightly dropped her mouth open.

Sal seized the opportunity and leaned in to kiss her luscious lips.

While Sal and Mae kissed, the bartender returned and said, "Here's your change."

Without breaking the kiss, Sal reached behind him with his free hand and held out his palm for the bartender to lay the money in.

He shoved the money into his trouser pocket while still embracing Mae.

Sal finally came up for air and left Mae breathless.

"Wow," she purred. "You can do that any time."

"You're a real looker," Sal told her. He ran a few fingers along her shoulder and down her arm. He dropped his gaze to her stockinged legs. "You have beautiful gams. Do you wanna dance with me?"

"I'd love to!" Mae exclaimed.

They left their drinks on the bar and Sal led her to the dance floor.

A bandleader dressed in a black suit and matching black bow tie announced, "Hey all you cats and kittens. What do you want to hear tonight? We have the best swing band in the city of Chicago." The large crowd in front of him cheered and whistled. "Wellman Braud is with us for a few nights. He comes to us all the way from the Cotton Club in Harlem with Duke Ellington." The bandleader motioned to a man holding a bow against an upright bass in the back left corner of the stage. The crowd erupted in applause again.

Sal squeezed Mae's hand as the bandleader introduced the rest of the members of his 17-piece band.

After a few hours of dancing to *Ain't Misbehavin'*, *Basin Street Blues*, and other songs, Sal led Mae by the hand out of the speakeasy and onto the sidewalk. The darkness of the city cast deep shadows from the few streetlamps nearby. Most of the city was quiet, letting sleep consume it.

Sal leaned into Mae, pressing her back against the building, his hand along her hip. "You're cute as a bug's ear," Sal said.

"I'm more than cute," Mae whispered, batting her eyelashes at Sal. Her mouth curved into a sensual smile.

"Don't I know it," he replied. He cupped her chin in his hands and lifted it upwards toward his. Sal kissed Mae, tenderly taking her lips in his.

"Do you wanna get outta here?" Sal suggested.

"Yes," Mae breathlessly replied. "My place is just up the block."

"Let's go." Sal winked.

With his arm around her waist, Mae directed Sal along hushed South Halsted Street. The flower shop and cold storage facility had closed for the night. A few night-prowlers wandered down the opposite side of the street.

Sal and Mae approached a three-story brick building on the next corner. Blue and white striped awnings blocked the first-floor windows. A bright sign attached to the main entrance read "P. Schiavone & Son - Bankers and Steamship Agents". The rest of the building was dark.

"This is my place." Mae nodded to the property. "I'm on the second floor."

She and Sal entered the vestibule, found the nearby stairwell, and made their way to the middle floor. Three units were in front of them.

They approached an apartment door marked with "2A". Mae pulled a key out of her pocket and unlocked the door. She opened the door and stepped inside.

"Come on in," Mae talked in a sultry voice. "We have the whole place to ourselves."

"Absolutely!" Sal pressed her against the wall and kissed her passionately. He lifted Mae into his arms. "Where's your bedroom?"

"Second door on the left."

Chapter 13

The next morning at Lou Mitchell's diner, Sal called to his favorite waitress. "Hey Thea, can me and Paolo get another cup of coffee?" He jingled an empty white mug in his hand as if he was ringing a bell. Paolo sat next to him at the counter as they ate platters of eggs, bacon, and sausage. Other patrons filled in the eating establishment; some of them were starting their journey on Route 66 heading out west.

"You got it, sweetie," Thea answered from the coffee station. A couple of carafes of the rich brew percolated beside her.

Paolo poked Sal in the rib. "How was last night? How was your date with Mae? Sorry I missed all the fun at the club. I had a few things to take care of." He shoved a piece of bacon in his mouth.

"I tell ya," Sal began, "Mae is a hot mama. We danced for a few hours. I bought her a few drinks. Then we went back to her place and made whoopee all night. She was still sleeping when I left her place this morning."

"How's she in--?" Paolo wanted to know. He made a double jabbing motion with his fingers.

"Mae's not like the other dames. She knows things I ain't never seen before," Sal answered. He gazed off over his friend's shoulder. "She's swell."

"Sounds like you're dizzy with a dame," Paolo deduced. "When're you seeing her again?"

"Hopefully this weekend. She can make me dizzy any time." Sal took a bite of his omelet. "But I gotta make some money first. Eddie finally called me about a job, so I gotta go see him after we're done here."

"Speaking of that," Paolo said, "how did your meeting go with Joe Aiello?"

"He's a tough bastard," Sal spoke in a whisper. "His goon squad was packing heat right in front of me. But it worked out okay. He lent me $50, but I have to do something for him."

"What does he want you to do?"

"He wants me to be like a stool pigeon and let him know when I know where Al Capone will be," Sal explained.

"How you gonna do that?" Paolo cocked a dark eyebrow. "It's not like you're running with him. Doesn't he know you're a simple college boy?"

"No idea," Sal sighed. "I'll figure it out. I have ten days."

Once Upon a Time in Chicago

* * * *

An hour later, Sal entered the law office of Eddie Devine. The middle-aged man, wearing a dark suit and a navy-blue tie, sat behind a massive oak desk. His hairline had seen better days. The back of his large, padded chair skimmed the edge of three expansive windows overlooking the south side of Chicago.

He spoke into his heavy black phone but acknowledged Sal as he walked in and motioned for him to sit in the chair on the opposite side of the desk. Sal sat upright in the chair.

"Yes, sir," Eddie said into the phone, "I think that's a great idea ... people are out of work, they'll need to eat ... you can set up one at Thanksgiving too, that's only two months away ... they'll wanna make you the new mayor of Chicago ... I'll get on the horn and tell the others and we'll get it set up." And he hung up the phone.

Eddie put his full attention on Sal. "Hey kid, I need your help with something, but we gotta keep it on the down-low. I'll pay you thirty dollas for it."

Sal quickly did the math in his head. Thirty dollars was a good start to pay back Joe Aiello, so he hoped he could get the rest before his deadline. "I'm all ears."

"Mr. Capone has this great idea to run a soup kitchen for all the people in the city who have lost their jobs this year," Eddie spoke. "You and me, we're lucky to still have one."

"Yeah, we are," Sal agreed.

Eddie continued, "He wants to show some charity and share the wealth. Do good for the local *paesans*. He wants to show them that he has a heart. We want to get it set up right away. I need you to help me to spread the word without saying who's behind it. We don't want the coppers staking out Public Enemy Number One. *Capisce?*"

"Yes, sir," Sal replied. He leaned forward toward Eddie's desk in anticipation.

"We want to give them coffee and sweet rolls for breakfast, and soup and bread for lunch and dinner. We won't deny second helpings and we won't ask anyone to prove their need. Capone can be the hero for the common man. The government sure isn't doing anything."

"What do you need me to do?" Sal asked. The idea intrigued him. He was sure that the unemployed already felt conflicted about taking charity from a well-known gangster, but maybe their rumbling stomachs trumped their pride and principles. A hungry man needed to eat.

"Go to Gonnella Bakery on Erie Street. Tell Ol' Man Gonnella I sent ya, and that we need 350 loaves of bread, 100 dozen rolls, 50 pounds of sugar, and 30 pounds of coffee. We need that much every day to feed all those people. Tell him he'll be greatly compensated for it. $300 a day should do it."

"Yes, sir." Sal stood from his chair and was about to leave when Eddie spoke again.

"One more thing, kid," Eddie spoke as he lifted a hand toward Sal. "Do you know a place with good minestrone? Mr. Capone wants to find a new place. Seems the regular joint he was going to stopped serving it. He asked me, but I didn't know because I went to the same joint."

"Yes!" Sal exclaimed. "Bella Napoli Cafe on South Halsted."

"Bella Napoli Cafe?" Eddie questioned with narrowed eyes. "That's a nice place. What were you doing there? On a date or something?"

Sal had to think fast. He didn't want his boss to know that he had met with Joe Aiello. If Eddie found out, Sal would be out of a job and in the lines for the soup kitchen. "Yeah," he lied.

"I hope she was worth that fancy dinner," Eddie joked. He raised a hand and sent Sal off with a wave.

Sal smiled to himself. He was thankful that Eddie didn't ask any further questions. He headed out the door to Gonnella Bakery.

Chapter 14

A week later, Sal sat on the stoop of his three-story flat on Shields Avenue counting the money in his billfold. The fall air lightly swirled around him, blowing a few rogue leaves down the street.

"Ten ... Twenty ... Thirty ... Forty ... Fifty ... Sixty ... Seventy ... Eighty," he said to himself as he thumbed through the stack of tens. "That's enough to pay back Joe Aiello and a little extra for me." He pocketed the money and exhaled, content that he met his mark and didn't have to worry about being fitted for cement shoes.

"Hi-ya, Sal!" Paolo called from a few yards down the block. "Whatcha doin?" Paolo strolled toward Sal and sat on the cement steps next to his friend.

"Just finished counting up the money that I owe Joe Aiello," Sal replied. He pulled a cigarette and a lighter out of his pocket and lit the *snipe*.

"How'd you come up with it?" Paolo wanted to know as he lit up his own cigarette.

"Eddie has me on a new job," Sal answered. "He's setting up a soup kitchen and I'm running all over the city talking to the suppliers."

Paolo stifled a laugh. "Is he having you bleed money from them?"

"No," Sal said. "It's not like that. These people are happy to help. Seems to be on the up and up." Sal took a drag from his cigarette. "He paid me $30 last week and $50 this week. More than I usually get."

"How much do you owe Aiello?" Paolo asked.

"Seventy-five," Sal said.

"Since you have an extra five spot, you wanna come with me to the game tonight?" Paolo asked. "I can save a seat for you at the table."

Sal considered the invitation. He was done with his studies for the day, so that freed up some time. If he was careful and bet low, he could play a few hands. Maybe even double his money and bring home ten or even twenty. "Sure, I'm in. What time?"

* * * *

At 9:00 that night, Sal swaggered into the back room of the speakeasy. Paolo waved him in and he took a seat at the poker table. The same players from the previous game stretched out around the table. A thick haze of cigar smoke filled the air. Various glasses of hooch cluttered the table.

"You came to join us again?" the dealer snickered through the cigar clenched in his teeth. "You didn't learn your lesson the last time, boy?"

The rest of the table howled in laughter.

"You taught me well," Sal countered with a sly grin. He exchanged five dollars for chips and stacked the paltry pile in front of him. He poured himself a full glass of whiskey.

"That's all you got? That's chump change," the dealer replied as he shuffled the deck and dealt everyone their hand.

Each player paid their ante of fifty cents into the center of the table. That left Sal with four and a half dollars in chips to bet. If he literally and figuratively played his cards right, he could last a couple of rounds and possibly take home some money.

"It's enough," Sal replied.

"You're one cocky S.O.B.," the dealer sniggered. "I will have a great time taking money from you tonight."

Sal slid his cards toward himself and snuck a peek. A jack, a nine, a six, a five, and a two. Garbage. He hoped the slight puff out of his mouth didn't give away his tell. He kept the six and the five in hopes of a straight and discarded the rest.

The dealer handed Sal three new cards: another six, a king, and a three. A pair of sixes and king high. Not bad, Sal thought to himself.

The large man to the dealer's left spoke, "Dolla." He tossed his amount of chips into the center of the table to start the bet. Paolo matched it as did everyone else between him and Sal.

"I'm in," Sal said as he threw his chips in the middle of the table. Even if he lost this round, he could still play another.

The bet came back to the large man and he grabbed a few more chips and threw them into the middle of the table. "Three dollas."

Paolo threw his money into the pile as did the guy next to him.

When Sal's turn came up again, he studied his cards and weighed his options. A pair of sixes wasn't much. "I'm out," he finally said and slapped his cards face down on the table.

The dealer snickered, "I knew you wouldn't last." He chewed on the cigar held tight in his fingers.

The rest of the players finished out the round and the large man to Paolo's right was the new dealer. He shuffled and dealt the cards as each of the other players paid their ante.

Sal pulled up a four of diamonds, a queen of clubs, a two of diamonds, an eight of spades, and a ten of diamonds. A partial flush. Not a bad second hand. He traded the queen and eight and received an ace of diamonds and a six of diamonds. A full flush. He took a swig of whiskey in hopes of hiding his excitement.

After two rounds of bets, the only two players left in were Sal and the gaunt man across the table from him. A nice pile of chips separated them. Sal had bet all of his money, a little confident of his hand but accepted the fate of the poker gods if he lost.

"Call," the thin man said. He laid out a three, a four, a five, a six, and a seven -- all of different suits.

A broad smile formed on Sal's face as he laid his cards face up. "I win." His dark eyes glowed in elation. He reached for the pile of chips in the center of the table and scooped them toward him. He wanted to throw the chips in the air like confetti but decided not to tempt fate with his gun-toting competitors. Sal quickly scanned the chips and counted approximately fifteen dollars. That would last him a few more hands.

The first dealer threw his cards down in disgust. "You got lucky, kid."

"Don't let 'im bother you," Paolo supported his friend. It was now Paolo's turn to deal.

Paolo handed Sal a king of spades, a three of spades, a five of diamonds, a jack of clubs, and a three of clubs. A pair of threes and king high. Another decent start, Sal thought to himself. He discarded the five and the jack. As he peeled back the two new cards, he tried to keep from smiling. A three of diamonds and a three of hearts. Four of a kind and king high. Sal's heart thumped inside his chest as he tried to show a bored face. Only two other types of hands could beat his: a straight flush and a royal flush. The odds were pretty slim that someone else at the table had a better hand than his.

The player next to Paolo tossed in a handful of chips. "Two dollars."

Everyone around the table matched it and Paolo doubled the pot.

Sal discreetly studied his hand and watched his opponents. Paolo scratched his nose a couple of times. The thin man sat stone-still, barely breathing. The large man puffed on his cigar as a bead of sweat curdled on his forehead. The rest of the players either shuffled in their seats or chewed on their fingernails. A curl formed on the side of Sal's mouth as his confidence increased. A gleam formed in his eyes.

After a few rounds of bets, the rest of the players folded and only Sal and Paolo were left. Sal knew that Paolo could hold his own but he had never been a big bettor. Sal expected not much more than a five-dollar bet from Paolo and one of them would have to fold. Sal didn't like to beat his friend but he would if he had to. This time it wasn't personal.

Sal scrutinized the four cards of threes in his fingers. He had never held such a good hand. The pot in front of him could be a good twenty-five dollars. That, and the upcoming money from Eddie Devine for the soup kitchen job, could last a few weeks.

Paolo pushed his entire pile of chips into the center of the table and wiped his forehead with his other hand. "Fifteen."

Sal quietly gasped as his friend bet everything he had. Maybe Paolo had a good hand. Sal glanced at his chips and counted them in his head. He had ten dollars left. Sal was pretty confident that he would win so he pulled five more dollars out of his billfold. Part of the money that he owed Joe Aiello. With this win, Sal would have enough to pay the gangster back and keep a lot for himself.

"I'm in," Sal said as he pushed all of his money into the center of the table.

"Call," Paolo said.

Sal laid down his four of a kind and a king. Paolo flipped over a two of clubs, a three of clubs, a four of clubs, a five of clubs, and a six of clubs.

"Holy crap," Sal exclaimed and slammed his fist on the table. "Paolo! I can't believe you did this to me!"

"You think I'd fold with a straight flush?" Paolo shot back. "I'm not an idiot!"

Sal jumped up from the table and startled the players sitting next to him, shaking their stacks of chips. "What am I supposed to do? I owe $75 to Joe Aiello!"

"Maybe you shouldn't have bet all your money," the first dealer snickered. "You fool."

"Shut up!" Sal shot back and pointed a finger at the man.

"Tell me to shut up again and it might be the last words you speak," the man replied. He slowly stood from the table, adjusted his suit jacket, and exposed a Smith & Wesson attached to his hip.

Sal slumped back in his chair when he knew he couldn't challenge the man.

The first dealer sat back down in his seat. "That's what I thought."

Paolo spoke to his friend across the table, "I'm sorry, Sal. I really am." He frowned at Sal.

"I gotta go," Sal muttered. He stood from the table again, downed the rest of his hooch, and stomped out of the room.

Sal stopped in the hallway of the speakeasy and collapsed against the wall. He was thankful that no one else lingered there. His heart thumped inside his chest. His breathing became more rapid and shallow. As he unbuttoned the top three buttons of his shirt, his hands trembled.

Where would he get the extra money? He was five dollars short to pay back Joe Aiello. His two weeks were up. Aiello would find him and his henchmen would break his legs. Or worse. He could ask his brother Phil for a five-dollar loan but he didn't want to tell Phil why he needed the money. Sal didn't want to involve Phil in his stupidity. His older brother teased him enough.

* * * *

Nightmares plagued Sal for the next week. He dreamt that Joe Aiello hunted him down in a dark alley and raised a Tommy Gun to his face. Greenbacks dangled in the air, just beyond Sal's reach. The blast of the bullet woke him up in a cold sweat, thankful that blood didn't fill his brain. His heart thumped, as the ominous demons tortured him.

What was he going to do?

Chapter 15

Two days later, Sal cowered at the furthest stool at the end of the counter of Lou Mitchell's diner. He slowly sipped a cup of coffee. It was all he could afford. Fortunately, Thea offered him free refills. He had avoided Paolo since the poker game and barely spoke to his family. His Ma and Pop had always believed in the faith of God, but Sal never held the same conviction. Maybe now was the time he needed a miracle. Where was a bowl of holy water when he needed it? He swirled a finger around the rim of the white cup sitting in front of him. Coffee wouldn't be a suitable replacement.

Thea had refilled his coffee cup and walked off to attend to other customers.

His two weeks were up. Sal owed Joe Aiello money and he was five dollars short. He accepted his fate and realized the next time he encountered Aiello and his henchmen, he might not breathe again.

When he left his house fifteen minutes earlier, Sal kissed his Ma and Pop goodbye, leaving them oblivious.

Sal gulped down his coffee.

A bell jingled on the exterior door and caught Sal's attention. Up until now, he hadn't noticed the small crowd of people in the diner having breakfast. Everyone looked up to the entrance and hushed their conversations as three men trekked inside. Two hired gunmen in matching black overcoats escorted Joe Aiello into the establishment.

Sal discreetly made a sign of the cross and kissed his fingertips as the three men approached him at the back of the diner.

"I came to collect my money," Joe Aiello commanded. His two henchmen stood stoic beside him.

Sal reached into his pocket and pulled out a stack of tens. "Here's what I have."

Aiello snatched the money out of Sal's hands and thumbed through it. "It's only seventy," he said. "You owe me seventy-five. Where's the other five? You stiffing me?"

His henchman sneered at Sal with killer black eyes.

"No sir. I'm sorry, Mr. Aiello. I would never stiff you," Sal replied. "I just couldn't get all of it."

"Well, what are we doing with you?" Aiello snickered and his goon squad laughed. The man on his left pulled a six-shooter out of his waistband and flicked the barrel. The ratchet sound chilled Sal's bones.

"Please," Sal pleaded. "Please give me one more day. I promise I can get it. Please."

Joe Aiello stepped around Sal and studied his prey. Sal sat motionless, unsure what he should do.

"Usually I don't allow extensions," Aiello stated, "but I like you, kid." His henchman put his gun back into his pants. Aiello spoke again, "You have 24 hours." He glanced at his watch. "It's 2:00 now, so you have until 2:00 tomorrow to pay me. But now you owe me ten. I will meet you here again tomorrow. *Capisce*?"

Sal swallowed hard and exhaled slightly. "Yes, sir. I promise you I will have it."

Aiello slapped a hand on Sal's shoulder. "Good answer." He turned and headed out the door with his bodyguards following a couple of steps behind.

As soon as they exited the diner, Sal puffed out a giant exhale and collapsed against the wall next to him.

"You gonna be okay?" Thea approached him with a fresh pot of coffee.

"For the next 24 hours I am," Sal replied. "You don't have an extra ten I can borrow, do you?"

"Not today, sweetie. I'm barely getting by as it is. A lot of people are out of work and I'm not as busy as I used to be." Thea refilled his empty cup. "This one's on the house."

"Thanks, Thea," Sal sighed. "I appreciate it."

Once Upon a Time in Chicago

* * * *

An hour later, Sal waddled into Eddie Devine's office. He gazed out the window trying not to give away that he was scared for his life. He nervously curled the cuff of his sleeve in his fingers. Joe Aiello's warning weighed heavily on him like a storm cloud that lingered in the distance. He knew the damage was coming, it was only a matter of when.

Sal pondered his options. He could ask his brother Phil, but Phil would give him a hard time about it. He could ask his sisters, but they'd want to know why and he wasn't ready to disclose his heathen activities. Pawning his parents' valuables was out of the question. He could ask Eddie for the loan, but...

"Hey, kid," Eddie's voice broke Sal's trance. "You did a great job with Ol' Man Gonnella. His bakery has volunteered to double the order for the soup kitchen."

"Huh--" Sal barely acknowledged him.

"I said Ol' Man Gonnella is doubling his order," Eddie repeated. "You keep doing what you're doing and I may have to give you a raise."

A slight grin curved on the corner of Sal's lips as he stood in front of Eddie's desk. He appreciated the offer, but he knew he wouldn't get the money in time to pay Aiello. His heart thumped inside his chest.

"That reminds me." Eddie reached into his pocket and pulled out his billfold. He opened it and held cash out to Sal.

"What's this for?" Sal squinted at the picture of Alexander Hamilton on the currency.

"It's yours. Take it," Eddie replied, flicking the money in Sal's direction. "I told Mr. Capone about your recommendation for the minestrone at Bella Napoli Cafe and he said it was the best soup he ever had. He even went into the kitchen and paid his compliments to the chef. He wanted me to give you this for the nice tip."

Sal's mouth fell open. He couldn't believe his luck. It was exactly enough to pay Joe Aiello. Ironic that it came from his biggest enemy.

"Thank you so much," Sal gushed, taking the money in his palm. "I appreciate it."

"You and I both know that ten dollars is pennies for Mr. Capone," Eddie joked. "He probably didn't think anything of it."

"But I sure do," Sal replied.

A monstrous breath exhaled his lungs.

Chapter 16

Later that afternoon, Sal joyfully skirted back and forth around his kitchen as his father directed him. Living at home gave him the freedom of a carefree lifestyle. Except for the money that he owed Joe Aiello, he had minor responsibilities. Sal had no reason to move out.

"Get pork and beef out of ice-a-box," Bartolomeo instructed. The elder Scavuzzo insisted on calling their modern fridge by its old name.

"What are we making, Pop?" Sal asked. Now that he had enough money to pay back Joe Aiello, he could enjoy spending the afternoon with his father.

"Spaghetti a la Scavuzzo," Bartolomeo boasted, kissing his fingertips and flicking them into the air. "I create it. Time you learn."

"Sure, Pop." Sal pulled the ground beef and pork out of the freestanding General Electric fridge and set it on the counter.

"Mash up two fistfuls of meat, then put rest back," Bartolomeo told his youngest son as he blended other ingredients in a large cast-iron bowl. "Then bring it here and I mix with your Mama's basil and parsley from her garden."

Sal dropped two large mounds of meat into the bowl as Bartolomeo added an egg, a handful of breadcrumbs, and a spoonful of salt. Even though Sal stood a good head taller than his father, Bartolomeo's commanding presence still intimidated him.

"This for meatballs," Bartolomeo said. "We bake in oven while we cook *madinad* sauce."

"Who's all eating tonight?" Sal asked, wondering if his brothers and sisters would join them.

"Everyone. Doesn't matter," Bartolomeo replied. "I make plenty."

Sal observed as his father blended all of the ingredients with his strong, calloused hands. Sal adored his father and admired that Bartolomeo worked hard for his family, sacrificing leaving them for a year so they all could start a new life. The years of hard work were evident in his Pop's hands.

Bartolomeo nodded toward the dry sink. "Get me metal tray."

Sal pulled a tin baking sheet out of a wide drawer and set it on the counter in front of Bartolomeo.

"Grab handful and make balls," Bartolomeo stated, cupping his hand to show Sal how small. "Like this."

As Sal helped make meatballs, he smiled wide, savoring this time with his proud father. Bartolomeo worked hard to support his family and they were lucky enough to have the things they did, especially when many *paesani* were out of work. After the duo filled the tray with spheres of raw meatballs and put them in the oven, they dropped garlic, oregano, pepper, onion, a pinch of sugar, and olive oil into a pan that had been heating on the stove. The concoction sizzled until everything formed a tawny color. Sal inhaled a whiff of the tantalizing ingredients.

He and his father added water, a half bushel of tomatoes, and more spices into a large pot. Then Bartolomeo poured the onion and garlic mixture in.

"Now we add secret ingredient," Bartolomeo directed. He stepped away from Sal and pulled a dark bottle out of the Hoosier cabinet. "Shhh. You tell no one." Bartolomeo held an index finger to his lips.

"Whatever you say, Pop." Sal grinned.

Bartolomeo uncorked the jug and poured red wine into the simmering pot of sauce.

"Where'd you get that?" Sal asked, knowing that his father couldn't easily purchase wine due to Prohibition. Sal knew Bartolomeo would never defy the law now that he was on American soil. He couldn't risk being sent back to Sicily or being thrown in jail and abandoning his family.

"I make it," Bartolomeo replied, pointing to the unlabeled bottle. "If you home, you know. I see when you not here." He glared at his son.

Sal cringed, knowing he couldn't keep everything from his Pop.

"Red wine is the secret ingredient?" Sal asked, purposely avoiding his father's statement. "Doesn't everyone know that?"

'No, *more* red *vino* is secret," Bartolomeo replied as he poured half of the bottle into the pot.

Sal laughed out loud. His father's dry humor never ceased to amaze him. Even though Sal stood taller, he always believed his Pop was the bigger man. The only time Sal witnessed his father cower was when Giuseppe Lombardo came to collect his money at the tavern years earlier. Bartolomeo had stood up to the city bullies ever since, despite losing his livelihood. The criminal underground ran rampant in the city, but the Scavuzzos avoided it as much as possible.

"It cooks three hours and we make pasta," Bartolomeo said. "One day, you cook this for your wife. She love you for it."

"But Pop, I'm not dating anyone right now," Sal protested. His father didn't need to know about Mae, even though he had plans to see her in a few days. Now that he secured money to pay back Joe Aiello, Sal loved his lifestyle. He could see Mae a couple of times a week and that left him plenty of time to play cards, go to class, and do a few jobs for Eddie. Bartolomeo's approval meant everything to Sal, even if that meant keeping his Pop in the dark sometimes.

"No matter," Bartolomeo replied, with a flick of his hand. "I make this for your Mama when I court her and we have six kids!"

Sal chuckled to placate his family-loving father. The duo couldn't be more different. Having a family didn't appeal to Sal. "Whatever you say, Pop."

Chapter 17

At 1:45 the next afternoon, Sal settled into his usual spot at the end of the counter at Lou Mitchell's. He sat upright and whistled a happy tune. With ten dollars in his pocket, he was confident about facing Joe Aiello again in fifteen minutes and come out unscathed. He came close to swimming with the fishes, but a combination of luck and opportunity saved him from that fate. Most of his life had been like that. His older brothers and sisters paved the way for parental inspection. He had coasted through his short adult life and was content. A thin line of arrogance formed along his lips.

"What can I get for you today, sweetie?" Thea approached him with an ever-present pot of coffee in her hand. "Some coffee?"

"Not today, Thea," Sal said. "I'm waiting for someone."

"Ah, right, the Big Shot, Joe Aiello," Thea smirked. She rested the carafe on a nearby burner and placed a hand on her curvy hip. "What are you doin' runnin' with him? You're a good kid."

"You know me, Thea," Sal protested, tapping himself in the chest. "I've been coming in here for years."

"Yeah, well, if you don't be careful with Joe Aiello, you might not be coming in here at all anymore," Thea warned. "He might take you for a ride."

"Don't worry, Thea," Sal smirked. "I can take care of myself."

"That's what I'm afraid of. I don't wanna be goin' to your funeral." She headed toward another customer, leaving Sal with his thoughts.

A few minutes later, a bell jingled on the exterior door as Joe Aiello and his goon squad entered the diner. Walking proud along the black and white terrazzo floor, they headed straight toward Sal.

Sal jumped off his stool and faced the well-feared gangster. He pulled the ten-dollar bill out of his pocket in anticipation of payment and held it upward.

"I see you found the money you owe me," Aiello said, his voice low and monotone. "I knew you would." He peeled it out of Sal's hands and inserted it into the inside breast pocket of his jacket.

"Yes, sir, Mr. Aiello," Sal replied.

Aiello studied Sal a moment before he spoke again. "You like working for Eddie Devine? How much does he pay you?"

"I do okay," Sal puffed out, unsure where the question was heading.

"How much?" Aiello repeated. His towering henchmen stepped toward Sal, raising the intimidation factor.

"I usually bring home forty dollars a week," Sal answered. A drop of sweat formed along his dark hairline.

Aiello smirked in Sal's face. "If your low down on Capone pans out, you come work for me and I'll double that."

Hot damn, Sal thought. He could buy a car with that amount of cash. Two cars. One for the daytime and one for nights out with Mae. Maybe even get his own place.

Sal held out his hand. "It's a deal, Mr. Aiello."

"Let's put a deadline on it," Aiello instructed, not yet accepting Sal's hand. "I want you to let me know something by the end of October. If you don't hear anything, the deal is off. *Capisce*?"

"Yes, sir, Mr. Aiello," Sal replied.

"I knew you were a good kid." He finally accepted Sal's hand. "I need to go to Rochester for a little while, but when I get back, I expect you to have something for me. You still have that business card I gave you?"

"Yes, sir, Mr. Aiello," Sal repeated.

Aiello and his triggermen turned and headed out the door, a silent cloud followed them. Sal barely had time to exhale.

"Salvatore Scavuzzo!" A woman's voice shrieked from across the diner.

Sal glanced up to see Thea barreling toward him, pushing her way past a handful of oblivious customers. She stopped in front of Sal, inches from his face.

"What are you thinking taking a job from Joe Aiello?!" she shrieked in a low voice as to not draw attention from other diners. Sal knew she didn't want to get him killed. She poked a finger in his chest, knocking him backward onto a counter stool. The buxom waitress had a few decades on Sal but she conjured enough adrenaline inside to best him. "You're a smart college boy!"

"He can pay me a lot of money," Sal protested. He still didn't dare push forward on his favorite waitress, even though he usually towered over her by a good six inches.

"I don't care!" Thea yelled, catching the attention of everyone else in the diner. The patrons hushed their conversations and watched the disruption to their dining on hash browns and eggs. "It was bad enough you borrowed money from him."

"But Thea--"

"Don't 'But Thea' me," she hollered. "I oughta go tell your Ma and Pop what you're doin'." She finally took a step away from Sal so that he could stand again.

"Thea, if I make more money with Joe Aiello, I can give you a big tip every time I come in here," Sal offered with a wide toothy grin. He knew he could charm the ladies with his good looks and wide smile and hoped that Thea would succumb to his wiles.

For a moment, she pondered his proposition. "No," she said, "I'm not taking any blood money from you. It's best to stay as far away from that dirty cash."

"It won't be like that," he said. "I promise you I will be okay."

"You don't know that. Joe Aiello is a bad man," Thea warned with a crooked finger. "If he wants someone dead, he finds a way. I cringe every time he comes in here to see you. I don't want to hear about you being gunned down in the middle of the street. Your Ma and Pop would be a wreck. They raised all of you to be good kids and sent you all to college and you're goin' to ruin everything they did."

Sal held the sexagenarian's hands in his, caressing her earned wrinkles.

"I promise you I will be careful."

Chapter 18

A few nights later, Sal laid in Mae's rumpled bed sheets, he in his boxers and she in his undershirt. The white cotton shirt engulfed her, covering her voluptuous body. Sal held Mae between his legs, drawing small circles along the soft skin of her forearm. She lounged against him, puffing a cigarette. They had spent the last couple of hours in the throes of passion.

Along with a few candles, a beam of moonlight spread light through the small room. The windows were cracked, allowing random sounds from the alley two stories below to spill in.

"I like you, Mae," Sal spoke. "You're swell. So pretty, too." He found a license to tousle her thick, long blonde hair through his fingers.

"I like you too, Sal," Mae replied as she pouted her lips and blew a puff of smoke into the air.

"Whaddaya say we go out?" Sal offered.

"We go out to the speakeasy all the time," Mae countered.

"Nah, I mean we go out for a nice dinner somewhere," Sal said. "Like to The Walnut Room. I hear they have great steaks."

"Oh, I don't know about that--" Mae said in a raspy voice.

"Why? Because you don't think I can afford it?" Sal protested. He lightly pushed her forward and twisted her shoulders around to face him. "I assure you I can afford it. I'll be getting the money."

"No hon, that's not what I meant," Mae said.

"Then what is it?" Sal wanted to know. He arched a dark eyebrow at her.

Mae ran a painted fingernail along Sal's freshly shaven chin. She shifted her body completely in front of him and leaned into him. On her body, his undershirt grazed his dark hairy chest. "I just like to stay here in bed with you," she purred as she planted soft kisses along his neck.

Sal disregarded her vague answer and focused on her sexy body. The power she held over him trumped any rational thought. He smiled wide and drew Mae into him, peeling his undershirt off of her...

* * * *

The next day, Sal walked into Lou Mitchell's for lunch. He could use a good BLT and a bowl of tomato soup. Thea wasn't around and Sal breathed a sigh of relief that she couldn't read him the riot act about Joe Aiello. After Sal placed his order with another waitress, he settled onto a counter stool and absorbed his surroundings. A man in a brown three-piece suit sat two seats over from him munching on a slice of apple pie a la mode while he read *The Chicago Daily News*. A pregnant woman and her young son nestled into a nearby booth eating meatloaf and a fruit cup.

The bell on the exterior door jingled as Paolo entered the eatery. He walked toward Sal and cautiously settled in the empty seat next to him.

"You still mad at me?" Paolo asked his friend, as he removed his fedora and placed it on the counter in front of him. "I'm sorry about what happened."

"Nah," Sal replied with a flick of his wrist. "That's old news. You're still my *goombah*."

"Good. I couldn't fold with that hand I had. Not even against you." Paolo offered his right hand to Sal. "I haven't seen you around in a while." Sal shook hands with Paolo, resealing their friendship. "Good, I'm glad. I missed hanging out with you. What's been happening?" He then ordered his lunch.

The friends ate as Sal caught Paolo up on everything that had been going on in the past couple of weeks.

"You did me a favor," Sal said as he ate a bite of his sandwich. "If you hadn't taken all my money at cards, Joe Aiello might not have offered me a job at twice what I'm making now with Eddie.

Aiello said he's gotta go to Rochester and then hopefully I'll talk to him again when he gets back."

"When's that gonna be?" Paolo asked.

"I dunno. He didn't say. I hope it's just a few weeks. Then I'll be bringing in the cash."

"You could buy yourself a Roadster with that kind of dough," Paolo chuckled.

"That's the plan," Sal replied. "I can see it now." He raised a hand and gazed off as if the luxury car was right in front of him. "Powder blue, a shiny chrome grille, stainless trim, and enough horsepower to cruise along Route 66."

"You gonna take your best *goombah* for a ride in it?"

"Of course," Sal boasted. "We could go all the way to California!"

Chapter 19

October 19, 1930

Sal hunched over an otherwise bare table pecking a typewriter in the front room of Eddie Levine's office. Eddie had given him a stack of envelopes to type addresses on, but Sal was no master of the anemone-like machine. What could have taken an experienced secretary 15 minutes tortured Sal for a good hour. Why Eddie never hired a woman to do this kind of task, Sal never knew. He could hear Eddie working and shuffling papers in the back room.

The phone in Eddie's office rang adding to the cacophony of Sal's tapping. He stopped searching for the correct key and listened for a moment.

Sal ignored the chatter until he heard the words, "Yessir, Mr. Capone." His heart jumped and he stopped typing altogether.

"That's great!" Eddie's voice carried into the front room. "I'll see you tomorrow night at Bella Napoli Cafe. 8:00."

Sal gasped as he realized he could give information to Joe Aiello about Al Capone's whereabouts. He quickly stood up from the desk and ran to the wooden coat rack in the corner of the room. He rummaged through the pockets of his overcoat and found the prize for which he was searching - the prize that could get him a car. A creased business card for the Chicago Sugar Supply Co.

Sal didn't dare call Joe Aiello from Eddie's office, so he shoved the card into the front pocket of his trousers.

Eddie emerged from the back room as Sal stood near the coat rack. "You done typing, kid?"

Sal froze. "No sir, just making sure I had gloves in my pockets," Sal lied. "It's getting cold outside."

"Ah, right. I saw the wind blowing out my window." Then Eddie nodded to the typewriter. "Let me know when you're done. I have another job for you."

"Yes, sir." Sal sat back down and Eddie returned to the back room.

As he hunted for the next set of letters for a mailing address, Sal grinned wide, imagining what else he could buy with the additional money working for Joe Aiello. A few suits from Marshall Field's. A gold watch. Leather shoes. And, of course, a new car.

Eddie had been a good boss, but money talked. Sal would be a crumb not to leave for more dough. He was pretty sure that Eddie would be fine without him, if not, maybe he would offer up Paolo as a replacement. Or even his brother Phil.

An hour later, after Sal finished the envelopes and handed them to Eddie, he scurried out of the back office claiming he was going out for a smoke break. He snatched his jacket off of the coat rack and rushed out the door.

Outside on the sidewalk, he pushed past people heading in and out of the deli in the adjoining building. At the next block, he ducked inside the lobby of The Palmer House Hotel. As bellhops and clerks shuffled by, Sal headed toward the bank of wooden telephone booths. He closed the glass-windowed doors behind him, dug into his pockets, and retrieved the business card and a couple of nickels. Sal lifted the receiver and dropped the coins into the five-cent slot. Even though it was unlikely anyone could hear him, Sal still glanced around to make sure no one in the hallway paid attention to the young man in the phone booth.

A telephone operator came on the staticky line. "What's the number?"

"SOU 8833," Sal replied. "Chicago Sugar Supply Company."

"Please hold."

As Sal waited for someone to pick up, his heart jumped. He couldn't decide if he was nervous or excited. After four rings, a man's voice answered.

"Yeah?" the man said.

"This-- this is Sal Scavuzzo," Sal stuttered, unsure of who he was speaking to. "I have information for Joe Aiello."

"Hold on," the man said, and then there was silence.

Sal wasn't sure if the man hung up or not but waited. Sal's knee bounced up and down nervously. He peered out the glass door, studying the crowd in the lobby. A bellhop wandered by carrying several suitcases but didn't take notice of Sal.

After a long, silent moment, the man came back on the line. "You can tell me and I'll tell him."

"Oh. Okay," Sal mumbled. He wasn't sure who the man was on the other end of the line, but he had no reason not to trust him. What was the worst that could happen? "Tell Mr. Aiello that Al Capone will be at Bella Napoli Cafe tomorrow night at 8:00."

"That all?" the man barked.

"Uh, yes... yes," Sal spoke.

"Okay," the man said, and then the line went dead.

Sal studied the receiver in his hand as if doing so could reconnect the line. He hoped the information would get through to Joe Aiello. He was banking on getting a lot of things with the money he would earn.

He exited the phone booth and headed back to Eddie's office.

* * * *

The next morning, Sal stopped to get a cup of coffee at Lou Mitchell's. As he settled onto his regular stool, Thea approached him, ready to take his order.

"Morning Thea," Sal practically sang to her. "How ya doin'?"

"I'm still worried about you," she grumbled. "You want some coffee this morning?"

"Yes, ma'am," Sal replied.

Thea grabbed a white cup from the stack of coffee cups piled on a shelf. She filled it with the hot brew and handed it to Sal. "Here ya go."

"Thanks Thea," Sal said, taking a sip. "That's the best coffee I've ever had. Your boss oughta charge more than ten cents a cup for it."

Thea chuckled. "I keep telling him that, but he refuses."

Sal laughed out loud.

"Speaking of money," Thea continued, "this is for you." She pulled an envelope out of her pocket and placed it on the counter in front of Sal. His name was written on the front.

"What is it?" Sal asked, staring at it in front of him.

"No idea," Thea replied. "Some big guy in an overcoat came in here an hour ago and said I needed to give it to you."

"Who was it?" Sal wanted to know, unable to guess who the man could be. He was a regular at Lou Mitchell's but did anyone besides Thea honestly pay attention to when he was there? He was expecting a payout from Aiello but didn't think it would happen at Lou Mitchell's.

"I don't know. Go on, open it." Thea motioned to the envelope still laying in front of Sal.

He snatched it up and tore it open under the counter. Sal's mouth fell open as he laid his eyes on the image of Ben Franklin on a crisp one-hundred-dollar bill. Cold hard cash. Enough money to buy a plane ticket to New York City. He had never been on a plane.

A business card dropped out of the envelope and landed on the floor, face down. Sal picked up the card, flipped it over, and read 'Chicago Sugar Supply Co.' on the front.

Sal locked eyes with Thea. "It's from Joe Aiello."

"Good golly!" Thea exclaimed, placing a hand to her heart. "You're in deep with him now."

"Don't worry, Thea," Sal told her. "I'll be okay. I promise."

Chapter 20

October 24, 1930

"Hey kid," Eddie called to Sal. "Come in here a sec."

"Sure thing," Sal hollered from the front room of the office. A half-empty glass of water sat before him. He had been busy sorting supply orders for the soup kitchen. Capone's plan had worked. The Organization was feeding two thousand people a day, with plans for more with Thanksgiving coming up.

Grabbing the glass of water, Sal trotted in the back office and found Eddie jotting some notes down. A smoldering cigar rested on an ashtray on the edge of his desk. Next to that, booze and ice cubes filled a highball glass.

"The last time you went to see Ol' Man Gonnella, how much bread did he give you?" Eddie leaned forward on his desk.

"Four hundred loaves," Sal replied.

"Tell him we need to double it for Thanksgiving," Eddie directed. "He'll have plenty of time to do it."

"When do you want me to see him again?" Sal drank a sip of his water.

Ring... Ring... The fat, black phone on Eddie's desk rang and interrupted them. Eddie snatched up the receiver.

"Yeah," he said into the phone. "Uh huh... uh huh... yeah... uh huh... okay, thanks for the low down." When Eddie clapped down the phone, an oversized grin kidnapped his face. "Hot damn! You're never gonna believe what happened."

"I--" Sal started to say.

"Joe Aiello is dead!" He slapped a thick hand on his desk, and Sal jumped back. "This is the best news I've heard all month. He was gunned down yesterday outside an apartment building on North Kolmar Avenue on the West Side."

The water glass slipped from Sal's hand and shattered on the floor. He rushed to clean it up, picking up the shards of glass. Averting his gaze, Sal obsessively scooped the glass into his hands. His future employer was dead and he willed himself to remain calm.

"Don't worry about it, kid," Eddie spoke as he grabbed a few rags from the corner cabinet to sop up the stray water.

"The West Side?" Sal managed to say, finally looking at Eddie, who was now on his hands and knees next to him.

"Yeah, apparently Aiello made a trip to Rochester and then was hiding out at that West Side apartment for the past 10 days," Eddie explained. "Mr. Capone's men were watching the place. Aiello wanted to move to Mexico and the guys found out and gave him a Scarface Special." Eddie cackled like an evil madman.

"They sure he was dead?" Sal wanted to know.

"I'd say so," Eddie answered as he stood up from the floor holding wet rags in his hands. "They pumped a pound of bullets into him. The meat wagon came, but he was already gone when they got to the hospital. The G-Men are on it, but nobody's talkin'. Now you know, but I suggest you don't talk either."

"I won't." Sal blew out a hard sigh as he put a hand on his knee as he rose from the floor. He raked a hand through his coal-black hair.

"You okay, kid?" Eddie asked. "You're too young to have aches and pains like me."

"Yeah," Sal lied. He couldn't believe the path to more money and a better life came to an abrupt halt. He had a lot of plans for all the extra dough.

"Mr. Capone's feud with him is finally over," Eddie added. "It's been going on now for five years. Aiello allied with Dean O'Banion to fight Mr. Capone early on. Then he joined forces with Bugs Moran and the North Side Gang. Word on the street is that Aiello had a $50 Grand bounty on Mr. Capone. At least 10 men tried to collect but ended up dead." Eddie chuckled again. "Goes to show you that we're with the right man." He tossed the dirty rags in a nearby trash can and walked back toward his desk.

Sal quietly gasped, not wanting to reveal his secret alliance with Joe Aiello.

"The funny part is that Mr. Capone didn't know anything about Aiello's whereabouts for a couple of weeks until four days ago," Eddie said as he picked up the highball glass that had been sitting on his desk, jingled the ice cubes, and took a swig.

"What happened four days ago?" Sal asked.

"When I met him for dinner at Bella Napoli Cafe," Eddie explained, "the chef told Mr. Capone that Aiello tried to bribe him with $10,000 to poison his minestrone. Then Mr. Capone's henchmen found out where Aiello was hiding out. They went after the man who threatened to kill their boss."

Sal's stomach dropped.

Chapter 21

As soon as Sal was done working with Eddie for the day, he hightailed it over to Mae's place. He climbed the stairs two at a time to the second floor, found apartment 2A, and rapped on her door. He needed to see her, feel her, be with her, and clear his head about the shocking death of Joe Aiello.

When Mae opened the door, she wore a green and white flowered day-frock that wrapped in a tie around her tiny waist. Her blonde hair fell in waves down her back. Her normally ruby stained lips were a matte pink. She wasn't wearing as much makeup as when Sal usually saw her, but he still found her pretty.

"Hi, Sal," Mae spoke quietly. "What're you doing here?" She peered over his tall body as if she was checking the empty hallway behind him.

"I need to see you," Sal replied. He stepped toward Mae, placed a hand on her waist, and nuzzled her neck.

"Not out here," Mae whispered as she led Sal inside and closed the door behind them.

Sal should have wondered why Mae was being so secretive, but he didn't. Like a stud racehorse with blinders on, he didn't have anything on his mind, except getting in bed with Mae. He grabbed her hand and led her to her bedroom. There, he bent down and scooped her up into his arms, and carried her to her bed.

Sal stripped down to his boxers and stood at the foot of Mae's bed. She laid in her bed still fully clothed.

"Your turn, sweetheart," Sal said. "Or do you want me to do it for you?"

Before Mae could answer, a sound at the front door caught their attention. They listened as someone jingled the knob and closed the door.

"Mae! Mae? You here, honey?" a man's voice called from the entryway.

"Oh my!" Mae gasped. "You have to get out of here!" She hurried off the bed and pressed any wrinkles out of her dress. "That's my husband!"

"What?!" Sal bellowed as quietly as he could. "Your husband!?"

"Shhh, keep your voice down," Mae whispered as she snatched up Sal's clothes from the floor and stuffed them into his open palms. She held his shoes in her hands. "You have to get out of here."

"Where am I gonna go?" Sal questioned, still in his boxers.

"Mae? Are you back in the bedroom?" her husband's voice grew louder from the hallway.

Mae glared at the window that led to the alley two stories below.

"No way," Sal protested as quietly as he could. His chest tightened at the thought of plunging to the sidewalk. "I'm not jumping out a window this high up. No way."

Mae herded Sal to the window. "My husband has a gun."

Sal's mouth fell open and he willed himself to keep from hyperventilating. He didn't feel like dying today and he didn't have time to think of another way out of Mae's apartment. As he raised the window frame with one hand, he held his clothes in the other. Mae tossed Sal's shoes through the open window and they clattered on the ground below. Sal scrambled out of the window as Mae kept a panicked eye on the door for her cuckold husband.

In an attempt to soften his landing on the cement sidewalk, Sal dropped his clothes to the ground below. He clung to the outside window ledge as he lowered his half-naked body, praying that nobody outside would see him. He eyed the unforgiving landing below and swallowed hard. If he was lucky, he would land on his pile of clothes and walk away with a few bruises. If not, he would die on impact and his poor parents would have to identify his shattered body.

As Sal's head dropped below the window threshold, he heard Mae's husband say, "There you are, darling. Did you hear me calling for you?"

Sal didn't wait around to listen for Mae's reply. He inhaled deeply, closed his eyes, and let his fingers slip from the window ledge. Missing his pile of clothes, he hit the cement on his feet with a thud and fell to his knees. Sal groaned but nothing immediately hurt. If anything was broken, he didn't feel it. He grabbed his nearby clothes, found his shoes a few feet away, and quickly pulled them back on. He straightened his clothes, caught his breath, and glanced at the window. He would never see Mae again.

Safely back in his clothes, Sal took off down the sidewalk. As he staggered home, a car nearly hit him. The driver cursed at Sal and shook a fist at him. Sal plopped down on the sidewalk and dropped his head between his knees, realizing what he had gotten into.

* * * *

When Sal found refuge at his family's three-story flat a half-hour later, he headed straight for his father's liquor cabinet and homemade wine. Fortunately, the house was quiet and Sal could drink in peace. Even though Bartolomeo's batch tasted more like grape-flavored vinegar, Sal didn't care.

He uncapped a bottle and held it to his mouth. As he chugged the vino, the day's events haunted his thoughts.

Mae was married. Married! How did he not know this? She didn't wear a wedding ring, but Sal knew of other women who didn't. He didn't think twice when he had previously asked her to go out for dinner and she insisted on staying in bed. His favorite place to be with her. After he encountered her on the street with Sophia, he didn't see Mae for a year. Did she get married then? Why did she never tell him?

Sal wiped a sweaty palm across his forehead and leaned against a nearby wall. He took another long swig of wine, finishing half of the bottle.

He couldn't see Mae anymore. No way. Before today, he was blissfully ignorant about her husband or that he carried a gun. Sal valued his life too much to fool around with a married woman whose husband could easily gun him down.

Sal knocked his head back and swallowed another mouthful of wine.

And Joe Aiello was gunned down. Killed on the street outside of his house. A man was dead because of Sal. He might not have pulled the trigger, but he initiated the events that led up to the murder. He chugged the remaining wine, rattled the empty bottle on the counter, and reached for a second jug.

What had he done? Would Capone's henchmen figure out that Sal had tipped Aiello off and come for him next? He would lose more than his job; he would lose his life. Sal shuddered at the thought.

Sal uncapped the second bottle and guzzled more wine. He wiped his brow as the booze burned his insides. Sal staggered to the kitchen table and plopped into a chair. His gangly legs fell awkwardly to the side.

Joe Aiello entered his mind again. The man was dead because of Sal. That would haunt him for the rest of his life.

As Sal swallowed more wine, he wondered how to get the cursed incident out of his mind. Sal hoped the answer was at the bottom of the bottle.

Chapter 22

"Hey, Sal, you in here?" Phil called from the front room.

Sal could hear his brother's footsteps getting closer, but he made no effort to respond from the kitchen table. He spun two empty wine bottles on the table in front of him, the whizzing motion mesmerizing his inebriated state.

"There you are," Phil said, as he entered the kitchen. "Did you hear that Ol' Lady Pappalardo passed a--" He grabbed Sal by the shoulders of his shirt and yanked him upright.

Sal bobbled his head a few times toward his brother, squinting his eyes as best he could toward Phil.

"Are you drunk?" Phil bellowed.

"Yes. Are you?" Sal's lips turned upward into a loopy smile.

"You twit!" Phil cursed his younger brother. "If Pop finds you in here like this, you're dead." He dropped his brother back into the kitchen chair.

"I'm already dead," Sal managed to say.

"What're you talkin' about?" Phil sat next to Sal, narrowing his eyes on him. "What did you do?"

Sal puffed out a quick sigh before he spoke. "Joe Aiello is dead." He spun a bottle in front of him again.

"Yeah, I heard. So?" Phil leaned closer to his brother and put a hand on top of the bottle to stop the spinning. "What's he got to do with you?"

"I killed him," Sal barely spoke above a whisper.

"What?!" Phil jumped up from his chair. "Where did you get a gun? Are the coppers coming here? Does anyone else know?"

"No... No..." Sal stuttered. "It's not... it's not like that. I'm not packing heat." He raised an unsteady hand and motioned to Phil's empty chair. "Sit down."

Phil took a seat again next to Sal.

"I didn't shoot him," Sal said.

"But you just said you killed him," Phil volleyed.

Sal rubbed his forehead, pressing out the stress that suffocated him. "He's dead... because of me... and Capone's goons are gonna find out... and come after me... So, I'm dead too."

"Hold on! YOU had Joe Aiello killed?" Phil pointed a finger at Sal. "You're some young *paesan* who lives on the South Side. How did you kill Joe Aiello if you didn't shoot him?"

Sal's gaze darted around the kitchen, focusing on something to form his response. He couldn't bear to meet his brother's disapproving eyes.

"I didn't mean to," Sal began, his head bobbing up and down. "Paolo... He hooked me up with Aiello... I needed money... Aiello said I'd be paid up... if I got him the low down on Capone."

"You're a scrub," Phil admonished his brother. "What were you thinking?"

"I wasn't," Sal sighed, remembering that Thea warned him of the same thing. "Then Aiello offered me a job... double what I made with Eddie."

"You still haven't explained how you got Aiello killed," Phil replied.

"I told Aiello where Capone would be..." Sal explained and inhaled a deep breath. "Bella Napoli Cafe... Aiello bribed the chef with ten grand to poison Capone's soup... The chef tipped off Capone and... Aiello got his own poisoning.... *Lead* poisoning."

"You think Capone is coming after you?" Phil deduced.

"Why wouldn't he?" Sal moaned, steadying his drunken gaze on Phil.

"Does he know that you tipped off Aiello?" Phil stated the obvious.

"No," Sal replied. "Only Aiello and the guy on his phone know it was me... But that doesn't mean Capone doesn't know. The snitch might sing like a bird if he's offered enough dough."

Phil shook his head at his brother in disappointment. "Here's what you're gonna do," he said. "You're gonna lay low for a while. A few months or so. Help Pop around the house. Teach Ma more English. Spend some time with Charlie and Rose and their families. The more time you spend here, the less likely you'll alarm anyone on the outside. Tell Eddie you need a break. If you need anything done, have Paolo or me do it. Stay away from the speakeasy and the cards."

"How'd you--" Sal started to say.

"I'm your big brother," Phil boasted. "It's my job to know everything you do."

Phil eyed the empty wine bottles in front of them and sniffed at his brother. "But first you're gonna clean yourself up before Pop finds you like this. Go wash up and put on some fresh clothes. You stink."

Chapter 23

February 1931

That night, Sal dreamt that Capone found out who slipped the info to Joe Aiello and gunned Sal down in the middle of the street. Sal had laid there, blood pooling to his sides and no one helped him. He lay dying and alone.

When he woke, Sal frantically patted his chest to make sure he was still alive. His hands shook like a woodpecker's head as he sopped the sweat from his face. He bolted out of his bedroom searching for something, anything, to help ease his fear.

Sal found his Ma sitting in the front room darning booties and he ran past her.

"Salvatore?" she called.

He ignored her and threw open the kitchen window, as he gasped for air. As he gulped in fresh pockets, his heart rate slowed. He couldn't live his life in fear like this.

* * * *

Sal heeded Phil's advice and laid low for the next few months. Eddie had agreed to let him take a break, causing a stall in his cash flow. He had already spent any money he had earned. Sal told Eddie that he would be taking a few months' hiatus so that he could focus on his family. Instead of going to the speakeasy, Sal spent evenings at home with his parents and siblings. They cooked together, played bridge and 500, listened to adventures of *Amos n' Andy* on the radio, and read the "Dick Tracy" comic strips.

As the nation gripped extra funds because of the Great Depression, Bartolomeo could no longer afford to send Sal to college. Without a job, Sal couldn't pay for it either and had to drop out.

Occasionally, Sal met Paolo at Lou Mitchell's to grab some coffee and catch up on the happenings around the neighborhood. When Sal had an extra quarter, they went to the cinema to laugh at *Animal Crackers* with the Marx Brothers.

On a cold and windy night in February, as Sal and Faye sat across from each other at the kitchen table playing dominoes, Phil wandered in with the evening newspaper clutched in his hand.

"Anything good in the paper tonight?" Faye asked her brother.

"Not much," Phil replied as he unfolded the paper and spread it across the table in front of his siblings. He pointed to a small headline:

Alvin 'Shipwreck' Kelly Sits Atop a 150 Ft Pole

"That guy is wacky. Who's dumb enough to sit on a pole?"

"He's smart enough to get himself in the newspaper," Sal replied.

He eyed another small headline while his siblings chatted about the man who sat on the pole for a month.

Capone Tried on Contempt of Court

Did this mean that Al Capone's reign could be coming to an end? Sal knew better. Capone had enough connections in the judicial system that he could make this trial go away within a matter of days. Sal witnessed it happen several times while working for Eddie. Coppers on the take looked the other way. Judges were slipped a few extra bills to find favor with the defendant or mysteriously misplace trial manuscripts. Witnesses disappeared or recanted on their prior testimony. Honest law enforcement found themselves frustrated trying to bring down the notorious gangster.

Sal was not oblivious to his indirect connection to the infamous mob boss and he had enjoyed the benefits. Now all of that was on pause. Maybe forever. Sal wasn't sure if he would work for Eddie again. Not until he felt safe. Not until he was confident that he wouldn't end up at the bottom of the Chicago River for relaying damning information to Joe Aiello. He shuddered at the thought. Being at home with his family was the best way to breathe. If he had to, he'd play games with his 20-year-old sister every night.

Bartolomeo entered the kitchen, interrupting his grown children. "I have announcement." He raised his arms above his stocky body, smiled wide, and pointed to his youngest daughter. "Faye, you to be married!"

"Oh, Papa!" She jumped from her chair, and embraced her father, splattering his neck and cheeks with kisses. "I'm so happy!"

"Your Nicholas ask me for your hand and I say yes," Bartolomeo said. "He good man for you."

"Congratulations, Faye." Sal and Phil hugged their sister.

"Nicholas is in front room waiting for you," Bartolomeo told Faye. "He has ring for you."

She broke her embrace and skipped out of the kitchen to her new fiancé.

"That just leaves you," Phil jested Sal and elbowed him in the ribs. "How's it feel to have your baby sister getting married and you have no one?"

"I ain't worried," Sal said. "There are plenty of dames out there for me." A smile formed on his lips.

"You don't call wife dame," Bartolomeo reprimanded his youngest son. "You *romanza*! You write love letters. You woo her." He held his hands up again and danced around the kitchen with an imaginary partner.

"Woo her, Pop?" Phil interrupted. "How do you know that word? It's American."

Bartolomeo stopped dancing and grinned wide at his sons. "I learn American words like you two." He proudly poked himself in the chest.

Sal barked a laugh. "You're dingy, Pop."

"So be it." Bartolomeo held his arms up once again and danced his way out of the kitchen.

"I think he's been putting too much wine in the sauce lately," Sal joked to Phil.

"Leave him be," Phil said. "He's just happy for Faye. When she gets married, you'll be the last one in the house. Ma and Pop will be setting you up with the girls from the church for sure." Phil snickered at his brother. "I hear that Mrs. Ricci's youngest daughter is single."

"Yeah, for a reason," Sal shot back. "She's got the face of a mule."

"You won't be so picky when you're 30 and still single." Phil stood up and scooped up his newspaper. "I'll see ya 'round. Joyce'll kill me if I'm late for dinner." Phil walked out the back door to home.

Sal pondered his brother's comments. He was 21 years old. He was the last single of his five siblings. Charlie, Rose, and Annie had several children of their own. Most of his cousins got married at this age. Many guys from the neighborhood had a wife and a baby on the way. Even though his Pop enjoyed it, Sal was still unsure about getting married.

After that fiasco with Mae, he couldn't be bothered with any dames at the moment. He hadn't seen her in four months - not since he jumped out her window. He still couldn't comprehend how he missed the signs that she was married. And why did she seek Sal out? Did she have no fear of her husband's gun? Maybe the bullet was never intended for her?

"Hi ya, Sal," Paolo called from the kitchen doorway. "Your Pop let me in. He's out there toasting your sister and her new fiancé."

"What're you doing here?" Sal asked. "Have a seat." He motioned for Paolo to sit at the table.

"I haven't seen you in a while and wanted to make sure you're okay," Paolo said.

"I'm good," Sal replied. "Staying in with my family. I told you that."

"The girls miss you at the speakeasy," Paolo said. "They heard you and Mae broke up and wanted to console you if you know what I mean." He winked at Sal.

"Maybe some other time," Sal said.

"What's wrong with you? Those sweet mamas want a piece of you and you're turning them down?" Paolo questioned. "You evil or something?"

"Nah, it's not like that," Sal said. Even though he and Paolo were thick as thieves, he couldn't bring himself to tell Paolo the real reason he'd been laying low. The less Paolo knew, the better. No need to bring his name into the muck and risk his life too. "I'm taking a break from the dolls, that's all."

"Well, if you change your mind, you let me know," Paolo offered. "You still taking a break from Eddie too?"

"Yeah," Sal said.

"How you bringing in the dough?" Paolo asked.

"I ain't," Sal sighed. He stood from the table, reached into his trouser pockets, and pulled them inside out.

"So, you're broke and celibate!" Paolo laughed.

"Don't rub it in," Sal said as he settled back down next to his friend.

"I can't help you in the sack, but I might be able to get you some dough," Paolo said. "It's small change, like ten, but at least it's something. You'll be able to meet me at Lou Mitchell's again for breakfast. Thea misses you."

"Maybe," Sal replied. He hadn't seen Thea in a few months because he didn't have the funds to eat out. "I don't want no trouble though."

"It's for my cousin Marco," Paolo said. "He needs someone to pick up a package from the train station."

"What kind of package?" Sal raised a dark, bushy eyebrow.

"I dunno." Paolo shrugged. "I don't ask him. He's my cousin. I trust him. You should too."

"I never met your cousin," Sal muttered.

"He likes to lay low," Paolo said. "Doesn't want anyone to put a face to his name. *Capisce?*"

"I dig you," Sal replied. He could empathize.

"You just go to the station office and tell them you're picking up a package for Marco. You don't even have to give your name. Once you get the package, get it to me," Paolo explained.

"How come you ain't doing it?" Sal asked.

"I can't," Paolo answered. "I have something else I need to do." He stared at Sal expectantly. "You in?"

Sal quickly pondered his options as he drummed his fingers on the table. He could use the money, even if it was a lot less than what he got from Eddie. It was a simple package and he wouldn't need to tell anyone his name so that Capone couldn't trace it back to him. How hard could it be?

"Yeah, I'm in."

"Good. Be there next Thursday at 7:00."

Chapter 24

At 6:00 the following Thursday, Sal paced his bedroom like a caged animal. He had an hour to get to Union Station, three miles north, via the trolley. With one hand, he jingled the keys in his trouser pockets, trying to ease his nerves. With the other hand, he pinched a cigarette between his fingers and exhaled a plume of smoke toward the ceiling.

Other than attending Sunday Mass at Santa Maria's with his family and the occasional trip to the grocer to get produce for his Pop, Sal hadn't left the house in months. He missed being out with Paolo and enjoying his life at the speakeasy, but also valued being alive. Even though Joe Aiello had been dead for four months, Sal's continued nightmares involved henchmen following him and gunning him down in the street. Just like Joe Aiello.

Sal checked himself in the mirror once more. He wanted to be inconspicuous. He hoped his gray overcoat and dark fedora would help him blend into the sea of other travelers at the train station. He couldn't risk a triggerman singling him out. Sighing heavily, Sal slipped on his shoes and headed out the door.

An hour later, Sal entered the Great Hall of Union Station. Brass lamps illuminated Bedford limestone Beaux-Arts facades and massive Corinthian columns. On the far end, near palatial windows, a double set of stairs led upward to other hallways. Myriad travelers scuttled around Sal. A husband accompanied his wife as he juggled her valises. A woman in a long, fur coat struggled to carry her overstuffed suitcase. Precocious children scampered around their parents, keeping themselves entertained while they waited for arriving trains. No one seemed to notice Sal.

He plodded up the marble staircase searching for the station office. He turned a corner, passed the restrooms, and a few yards down, read a sign hanging from the ceiling saying "OFFICE." Keeping his head low, Sal hugged the wall.

He stood at the entrance of the office and rapped on the glass window.

"Come in," a gravelly male voice instructed.

Sal twisted the knob and slid inside the small room. A man old enough to be Sal's father hunched behind a wooden counter. Stacks of boxes and files tottered behind him on a table. The man coughed several times and he pulled a handkerchief out of the breast pocket of his jacket.

"Can I help you?" the man asked. He coughed again, still using the heavily soiled handkerchief.

"Hi, I'm--" Sal began, almost stating his name. "I mean, I'm here to pick up Marco's package. Do you have it?"

"Yeah, I got it here somewhere." The man turned away and coughed a third time. He ran a finger over the boxes on the table, studying the recipient names. "Ah, here it is." More coughing.

Sal pushed his nose toward his coat lapel and assumed the man had tuberculosis.

The old man grasped the medium-sized, brown wrapped package in his hands and set it on top of the counter in front of Sal. "Here you go, young man." He coughed again.

"Do I have to do anything else?" Sal questioned, taking the box in his arms.

"No, that's all," the man replied. "Unless you can get me a new set of lungs."

"I'm sorry I can't," Sal said. "Have a good night." He nodded his head in commiseration.

As Sal carried Marco's box through the hallway, down the staircase, and through the Great Hall, he wondered what was inside. The box was heavy enough to use two hands, but Sal wasn't straining himself. Nothing inside rattled or ticked. Despite his curiosity, Sal didn't peek inside the box.

As he stepped outside and headed toward the trolley stop, a sigh of relief overcame him. As far as he could tell, no one outside noticed him.

"Excuse me, sir," a male voice called from behind Sal.

He ignored it, hoping that the owner was talking to someone else. Sal continued down the sidewalk.

"Sir, excuse me," the voice grew louder.

Sal couldn't risk anyone stopping him and kept walking. The heavy weight of the box felt like a dozen bricks and he tripped over an uneven section of pavement.

A hand grabbed Sal's overcoat, forcing him to come to a halt. He blew out a nervous sigh and gazed downward, hoping the brim of his fedora covered his face.

The hand belonged to a policeman dressed in a navy-blue uniform. Light from nearby streetlamps gleamed off a dozen brass buttons that fell in two columns running down his round chest. He wore a matching peaked cap.

"Excuse me, sir," the police officer repeated. He motioned to the package in Sal's hands.

Instinctively, Sal shifted the box away from the police officer. He swallowed hard and discreetly glanced around his surroundings. He had nowhere to hide in the crowd that wandered by. If he ran off, the copper would surely chase him down and charge him with resisting arrest. Sal's heart hammered inside his chest, assuming this was the moment that would land him in the clink. He felt faint. His

Ma and Pop would never forgive him. The box weighed heavy in his hands as if it understood the circumstances.

"I stopped you," the police officer began, "to see if you needed assistance carrying that package on the trolley."

"What-- Oh--" Sal stuttered, relieved that the copper did not want to arrest him. "No, I'm fine, Officer. I can handle it myself."

"Okay, just making sure," the man replied. He nodded and smiled at Sal. "Have a nice evening."

"You too, Officer," Sal said.

As the policeman wandered off down the street continuing his nightly duties, Sal blew out a colossal sigh of relief.

"That was close," he muttered to himself. As Sal's heart returned to its normal pace, he gripped the box tightly and headed toward the trolley stop.

* * * *

The following morning, Sal opened his front door and let Paolo in. As they settled on the couch in the front room, they lit up some cigarettes.

"Did you get the package for Marco?" Paolo asked.

"Yeah." Sal blew a thin cloud of smoke out of the corner of his mouth toward the ceiling.

"Everything go okay?" Paolo spoke out of the side of his mouth.

"Yeah, the guy in the office handed it right over without question," Sal said. "Didn't ask for my name or nothing. Some *medigan* could've picked up the box and the man wouldn't have known."

"Other than that, you were fine?"

"Once I left the train station, a copper stopped me," Sal explained. "Nearly shit my pants. I almost started praying to the Blessed Mother. But he just wanted to help me out on the trolley. Not sure if I want to do anything like that again. I almost pissed myself."

"Lucky you. You didn't open it, did you?" Paolo asked.

"Nah, it's in my bedroom," Sal said, nodding down the hall. "That way my Ma and Pop don't ask questions."

"They ain't here?" Paolo glanced around the flat.

"They're up at the church with Faye meeting Father Lazzeri," Sal said. "Planning Faye's wedding in June."

"Okay, then go get the package for me," Paolo directed. "I have your money." He reached in his pocket, pulled out two Lincolns, and waved them in front of Sal.

Sal got up to retrieve the package and carried it back to Paolo.

"Here ya go, pal." Sal placed the box on the sofa in between them. He pulled the money out of Paolo's fingers and stuffed it in his pocket. "I can meet you for breakfast at Lou Mitchell's tomorrow."

"Plan on that," Paolo said. "Thea told me she misses you." He stood up, lifted the box from the sofa, and headed toward Sal's front door.

"Do you know what's in it anyway?" Sal nodded to the package as he held the door open for his friend.

"I learned sometimes it's better if you don't know these things," Paolo warned.

Chapter 25

April 1931

Sal headed out the door of his flat. The mid-spring day was cool and damp. Heavy drops of rain patted on the metal roofs, reminding Sal of the gunfire that he had heard two years earlier on the north end of the city. Sal raised the collar of his jacket and pulled his fedora low over his ears to protect him from the wet breeze.

As he wandered north along Shields Avenue, rain dripped off the brim of his hat. The putrid stench from the Stock Yards made him gag. He would never get used to it. The only way to smell fresh air again was to move out of Chicago, and Sal had no reason to do that.

In a nearby alcove, a youngster in a newsboy cap clutched a pile of newspapers in his hands keeping his daily gold dry. He shouted,

"Hot off the presses! Get today's news! Five cents! See *The Public Enemy* at New Palace Theater!"

The juvenile entrepreneur's last statement caught Sal's attention. He had overheard chatter about the movie; a film about a young man's rise in the criminal underworld in prohibition-era urban America. The plot intrigued him. He had some time on his hands and headed toward the trolley stop for New Palace Theater.

On the trolley, Sal angled past a young family and took a seat on the hard bench. The moppy-haired little girl caught his eye; the sweetness in her innocent face calmed him. He watched her as she sat on her mother's lap, taking in everything around her. Sal had spent time with his nieces and nephews, but this tot fascinated him. She made him think about settling down with a good woman and starting a family. Maybe someday. He needed to figure out his life first.

When the trolley stopped a block away from New Palace Theater, Sal disembarked and followed the crowd to get in line for the movie premiere. The rows of golden lights on the marquee shined bright enough to land a zeppelin. Ornamental cast iron baluster panels bordered the top of the marquee. In the center, more gleaming lights illuminated the word "Palace". On the side, big block letters read: James Cagney & Jean Harlow in *The Public Enemy*. The bright cinema could be seen from several blocks away.

As Sal and the rest of the line plodded toward the ticket window, the rain softened to a light mist. Finally, Sal found himself at the ticket window, facing a pleasant-looking man behind a wall of glass.

"One, please," Sal said.

"Twenty-five cents, please," the man replied.

Sal reached in his pocket, found two dimes and a nickel, and exchanged them for a ticket.

"Thank you, sir," the man said and pointed to the side. "Enter through the door to your right."

With his ticket in hand, Sal followed the rest of the moviegoers into the main seating area. Above him, complex golden arches and brass ornaments highlighted the French Baroque architecture. It reminded Sal of the photos he had seen of the Palace of Versailles in France in his college world history class. He settled into a red velvet chair as the screen curtains opened.

Eighty-three minutes later, the movie ended and Sal was filled with dread as he staggered out of the theater. He had laid low for a few months now and kept out of the crosshairs of Al Capone. Sal believed the rumors that Capone ruled through viciousness, ferocity, brute force, intimidation and fear. Was it Sal's destiny to end up like James Cagney's character? Dead. Compliments of the mob.

* * * *

The next morning, Sal stopped at Lou Mitchell's and found an empty stool at the counter. He sat between a young man reading a newspaper on his left and an older gentleman on his right slowly sipping a cup of coffee as if he was delaying death.

"What can I get for you, sweetie?" Thea asked him. She held a steaming pot of coffee in her hand.

"Just some coffee." Sal nodded to her pot.

Thea grabbed a clean, white cup and saucer from a stack behind her, placed them in front of Sal, and poured a stream of ebony liquid into the cup.

"I've been meaning to tell you. I'm not one to wish ill will on anyone," Thea stated, "but I'm glad Joe Aiello is dead. He was a bad man." She wagged a finger at Sal. "You were lucky that you didn't get in too deep with him."

"I know, Thea," Sal sighed. "Believe me, I know." Sal was happy that she didn't know that Capone might still be after him or she might put a curse on him. He felt bad enough; he didn't need Thea's hex too. Even though it had been six months since Joe Aiello was gunned down, Sal still didn't feel safe. Wronged men never show mercy. Especially in Chicago.

The young man on Sal's left interrupted their conversation. "Did you see this?" He laid down the *Chicago Tribune* flat on the counter so that Sal and Thea could see the headline:

Five Seized in Raid on Capone's Stills; Alcohol Stock Taken

"Says Eliot Ness led the raid and destroyed $500,000 worth of hooch." The man pointed to the black-and-white copy. "Who the hell is Eliot Ness?"

"He's a nobody," a man's voice bellowed from behind them. "It was pure luck."

Sal turned to see Eddie Devine striding toward him. Eddie spoke again, "How ya doin', kid? I haven't seen you in a while. I thought I might find you here. We need to talk. *Capisce?*"

Sal's stomach dropped and his palms broke into a cold sweat. He was a dead man. He was sure of it. Eddie had come to take him right to Capone. Laying low wasn't good enough. Capone had figured it out. Sal was sure of it.

"Yes... sir...," Sal stuttered.

Eddie grabbed Sal's elbow and led him away from the counter, leaving Sal's cup of steaming coffee behind.

With a tensed jaw, Sal didn't dare glance back at Thea. She had warned him and he let her down. He felt like he was being led to his execution. Would Eddie bring him to a man who could fit him for cement shoes?

When they passed through the doorway, Eddie stopped Sal on the outside wall of the diner, near the aluminum and glass storefront. The red neon sign above them for Lou Mitchell's gleaned against the sunlight. Nearby, a small crowd of people strolled down Jackson Boulevard, packages in arms. He imagined himself running through them to escape.

Sal gulped, readying himself for the worst. He had wished he told his Ma and Pop that he loved them when he left the house that morning.

"Please... Please... I'll do anything..." Sal held his hands up as if he was praying. Even though Eddie was a few inches shorter, Sal still felt like a cornered mouse.

"What? What are you doing?" Eddie clapped back. He tilted his head at Sal, his fedora nearly falling off his head.

"I'm such a twit," Sal said in a low voice.

"Huh?" Eddie said. His hand slapped Sal with a hearty smack on the cheek. "You're acting wacky, kid. I brought you outside because I wanted to talk to you privately about your job. Didn't think you wanted the whole diner to hear our conversation."

Sal's shoulders relaxed and he lowered his hands to his sides. He silently exhaled knowing that his execution had been stayed.

"What about my job?" Sal wondered.

"I know you needed some time off to spend with your family," Eddie began, "but after seeing that newspaper headline today, I don't want you coming back. It's not safe."

"But you just said inside that Eliot Ness was a nobody." Sal furrowed his dark brow in confusion.

"I said that to appease the masses," Eddie explained. He stepped closer to Sal, closing the gap between them. "For years, he couldn't be stopped and anybody arrested in The Outfit walked scot-free. But nobody on the outside needs to know that Mr. Capone's Organization is now feeling the heat. *Capisce*?"

"Yessir," Sal replied.

Eddie continued, "Mr. Capone is concerned. He lost a lot of dough this week. He's tightening the pockets and closing unnecessary books. I can't have you work for me again. You did a great job, but you're a good kid. I want you out of the crossfire. I want you to live a long life and that might not happen if you come back. You might end up in the clink. Or worse."

Sal knew exactly what Eddie meant.

Eddie reached into his pocket and grabbed his billfold. He pulled out a twenty and presented it to Sal. "This is for you. Consider it your goodbye present."

"Thank you, Eddie." Sal took the money and slid it into his pocket.

"Take care o' yourself, kid. *Abyssinia.*" Eddie tipped his hat at Sal and headed off down the street.

Chapter 26

Sal wandered back inside Lou Mitchell's and found his cup of coffee still steaming on the counter. Relieved by the unexpected turn of events, he plopped down on the barstool in front of Thea. His heart rate had returned to normal and he released the breath he had been holding. A smile formed on his lips as he raised the coffee cup to his mouth. The two men who had been sitting there were gone.

"What happened out there?" Thea leaned on the counter and nodded toward the door. "When you left with Eddie, you looked like you were heading for your grave."

Sal lowered the cup to the saucer. "I'm out of a job," Sal said, curtly.

"How is that good news?" Thea questioned. She stood upright and placed a hand on her curvy hip, staring at him imperiously.

"It ain't," Sal replied. "I need to find another. Do you know anyone hiring?" He was hopeful that Thea could find him something legitimate.

"I don't, sweetie. That will be tough around here," Thea said. Her soulful eyes burned into Sal. "There are lots of people out of work and at the soup kitchens." She nodded to the partially filled tables and red padded booths behind Sal. The booths' adjoining coat racks lacked jackets. "This place used to be packed. If people aren't working, then they aren't coming here to eat. I'm lucky to still be here."

"But you should be happy. I cut all ties to Joe Aiello AND Al Capone!" Sal tried to keep his voice down.

"Good, I'm glad," Thea replied. "Now I won't have to worry about you being gunned down in the middle of the street." She placed a hand that had served thousands of cups of coffee to her heart.

"What's good today?" Sal changed the subject, nodding toward the kitchen area. "I'm hungry."

The owner, William Mitchell, who named the eatery after his son Lou, hunched over a dozen eggs sizzling on the griddle. A few cuts of bacon hissed on the top corner of the hot flattop. He wiped a large hand across his forehead so that his sweat didn't drip onto the griddle and splatter with the grease.

Thea answered, "He's got breakfast going now, but he can make you a club sandwich if you like. The Greek bread was made a few hours ago."

"I'll take the eggs and bacon," Sal said. "And a coupla pieces of toast while you're at it."

"I thought you were out of a job?" Thea arched an eyebrow at him.

Sal pulled the twenty out of his pocket and slapped it on the counter. "My breakfast is compliments of Eddie Devine."

* * * *

With a full stomach and nineteen dollars in his pocket, Sal headed out the door. Even though his breakfast was only sixty cents, he was feeling generous and gave the rest of the dollar to Thea for a tip. Without a job, he wasn't sure when he would see her again. She had been good to him and he wanted to compensate her for it while he could.

Sal wandered east along Jackson Boulevard, toward the Chicago River. He needed to clear his head and the majestic water could help him. He had just escaped death. The shrill of whistles filled the air as trains headed to Union Station a block away. He pulled his jacket tight to shield himself from the cool breeze.

Across the street from Sal, a disgruntled crowd stomped the sidewalk hoisting signs above their heads that read "We Want Beer!"

The protestors wore trench coats over their three-piece suits as similarly dressed supporters rooted them on.

Even though the 18th Amendment had been in place for over a decade, Chicagoans still demanded their libations. Sal had been lucky to visit the speakeasy to imbibe, but he knew some locals weren't as fortunate. He hadn't been there in several months, and he wasn't sure when he'd be back. With the current state of his cash flow, that timeframe seemed to be in the distant future.

As Sal passed the mass of people, he observed what had fueled the protest. Three police officers clad in navy-blue and brass uniforms stood guard as two men in straw hats and rolled-up sleeves dumped a barrel of amber liquid onto the street. The beer spread into the cobblestone crevices, forging tributaries along the smooth brick.

A couple of minutes later, the Chicago River came into Sal's sight. The untamed ripples sparkled in the late morning sun. Half a dozen black iron rolling bridges lined the riverbanks, simultaneously open for the barges, tugboats, and ferries to chug through. The onshore piers and docks were filled with sweaty and tired workers loading and unloading cargo all day. Across the river, a massive neon sign for the Majestic Hotel touted in-room radios and refrigerators. Factory whistles blared in the distance.

Sal stepped between two parked black Roadsters and strode toward the end of the sidewalk at the river's edge. He leaned against the rail and joined nearby onlookers observing activity on the dock below them.

Twenty feet down, men in tattered clothes and greasy hats hauled hulking bags of sugar and grain on their shoulders to eventually reach bakeries and restaurants. Cranes lifted crates of boxes from ported barges to waiting trucks. A few men in overalls perched on empty containers smoking cigarettes.

"Look down there!" Someone shouted from the crowd around Sal. An uproar of curses and thumping sounds came from the dock below. The rubberneckers near Sal jockeyed for position figuring out what the commotion was.

The crowd gasped and gawked as two men on the docks threw punches at each other. The bigger one knocked the smaller one to the ground, blood trickling from his nose onto the soiled pier. "That's for stealing from the pile." The larger man scoffed at his victim and walked away.

"That guy got off easy," the man next to Sal added. "I've heard some dockworkers getting shot if they get caught skimming off the top."

Sal knew of a few people who performed the manual labor, but this was the first time he witnessed someone get slugged because of it. He constantly read signs soliciting dock jobs, but he wanted no part of it. The paltry pay wasn't worth the bloodshed.

He abandoned the crowd and headed home. He was lucky he had food to eat and a roof over his head, optimistic that he would find a job soon.

Chapter 27

May 1931

Spring in Chicago not only brought out warmer temperatures and blooming flowers but also saw trolley lines full of drying laundry strung between the backs of buildings. Proud Chicagoans didn't want their neighborhood to see their clothes hanging in full view. Fluffy, white clouds pushed slowly across the vivid blue sky as if they had no particular place to be either.

Sal stepped off his porch, leaving his jacket inside for a colder season. He wore a white button-down shirt, black suspenders, and navy-blue trousers. Feeling rebellious, he left his coal-black hair uncovered, even though his Pop always told him to wear a hat because it was the proper thing to do, regardless of the weather.

He planned to meet Paolo at the next corner.

Several other people wandered down Shields Avenue passing Sal. A small crowd formed around a street musician who played a music box grinder for the dancing monkey on his shoulder.

Sal wandered past a barbershop and ran a hand through his thick hair, contemplating a cut. The men inside laid on reclining chairs with white towels steaming their faces. Barbers hunched over them, straight blades in hand, ready to shave. Sal decided to forego a haircut because Paolo was waiting.

A few cars and trolleys rumbled down the street, their horns and bells adding to the melody of the busy afternoon.

Sal could see Paolo at the end of the block, dramatically dickering with a grocer about his bananas in a nearby barrel. Sal became fixated on his friend arguing with the grocer.

As Sal stepped off the curb and into the street, a car horn "aoogha'd" at him. Sal jumped back, stumbling onto the sidewalk. His elbow scraped the pavement as he fell, tearing a hole in his shirt. He held his arms to his chest as if to protect himself from the steel machine.

"You have to be careful! I could have hit you!" The young female driver yelled from her black Humber Snipe. She had lowered the fabric roof of the car and her blonde curly hair gleamed in the mid-afternoon sun.

Still shaken, Sal took his time rising to his feet. He studied the young woman as he found his bearings again. She wore a red dress that had tiny white polka dots scattered all over it. White gloves covered her hands and extended to her elbows. A matching white, wide-brimmed hat lay next to her on the leather bench seat.

"I'm so sorry…" he started to say as he approached her vehicle.

"No, I'm sorry," she said. "I almost hit you. Are you okay?"

"Yes," Sal said. He rubbed a hand along his other elbow. "A little banged up, but I'm fine."

"My father would have been so upset with me if I hurt you," the young woman said in a near whisper. "This is the first time he's let me drive this car without him."

"I'm fine. Really," Sal repeated. Sal gazed into her pleading blue eyes. She had an innocent soft face, not at all like Mae's worldly one. It'd been so long since he'd been around a nice young lady that he forgot what he wanted to say.

"Good, I'm glad." She placed her gloved hands at the top and bottom of the large steering wheel. The car, obviously built for a sizable man, dwarfed her tiny body. Sal liked the way she looked in it. She had sweet confidence about her.

"I'm Sal." He reached his hand over the car door and waited. The young woman slowly let go of the steering wheel and accepted his hand.

"Dottie."

Sal chuckled to himself, amused that her name matched her polka dot dress. He hoped she did it on purpose so that people remembered her. He knew he would.

"Good to meet you, Dottie," Sal replied. "Do you live around here? I haven't seen you around."

"On the West Side," Dottie said.

"What are you doing here on the South Side? This is out of the way for a pretty gal like you," Sal spoke. In the middle of the street, he leaned against her pristine car door, making himself comfortable.

Dottie sat taller in her seat, giving Sal the impression that she was unsure of his charming advances. He peeled himself from Dottie's car, stood upright, and stepped back, not wanting to scare her away. She intrigued him and he wanted to know more about her.

"I'm on my way to-- Oh, I can't tell you," Dottie caught herself. She pulled her gloved hands closer to herself as if she was hiding something.

"Why not?"

"Because my father warned me not to talk to strange men."

"I'm not strange," Sal said. "We shook hands and you know my name." He ran his thumbs under his suspenders as he puffed out his chest.

"I don't think my father would approve of me talking to a man I met on the street," Dottie said.

"Maybe I need to meet your father," Sal offered.

Suddenly, another car horn blared before Dottie could respond. She and Sal looked back at the car waiting behind her.

"I should go before that driver gets mad at me," Dottie said. "It was nice meeting you, Sal."

She lifted her foot off the brake, exposing her stockinged legs, and put the gear shift in drive, leaving Sal alone on the sidewalk.

"Nice meeting you, too," Sal said to himself. He stared as Dottie drove down the street, out of sight.

"Who was that?" Paolo raced up behind Sal, out of breath.

"Dottie," Sal answered, still wistfully gazing at the street where she had once been.

"Who's Dottie?"

"The prettiest gal on the West Side," Sal said, finally facing Paolo.

"The West Side?" Paolo scoffed. "You'll never see her again."

"That's okay," Sal said. "She can come visit me in my dreams." Even though he only talked to Dottie for a few moments, the brief conversation gave him enough swagger to talk to dames again. Ever since he jumped out Mae's window, he felt he had lost his touch.

"Even if she did live around here, you can't afford to take her anywhere," Paolo added. "You don't have a job."

"You're right." Sal knew his friend had a point. "A pretty gal like that deserves a man with a job. She probably comes from money since she's driving around in a tin can like that."

"You said it," Paolo agreed.

"The only thing I've seen open are jobs down at the docks. And I ain't working down there," Sal said. He hooked a thumb north toward the river.

"Yeah, my cousin Marco knows a few people down at the docks," Paolo explained. "He said you gotta be plenty rugged to work down there. Lots of grifters and greaseballs hanging around too."

"That's no place for me," Sal said as he smoothed a hand along his button-down shirt and clean trousers. "I need to find something else."

"If you are interested, I can ask Marco if he has any more small jobs for you," Paolo offered.

"Yeah, I need something," Sal sighed. "Especially if I meet another sweet gal like Dottie again."

Chapter 28

June 5, 1931

Two days before Faye's wedding, the Scavuzzo household bustled making final preparations. Faye was in the kitchen with her mother and sisters baking cookies and twisting fried dough powdered with sugar. The room filled with sweet aromas of almond and vanilla.

Sal joined his father and brothers in the front room, trying on their dark suits to make sure they fit. Bartolomeo had pulled out a large oak mirror from the bedroom and rested it against the wall so that the men could check their fittings. A dozen black and white family portraits hung on the opposite wall.

"You ready for your youngest daughter to get married, Pop?" Sal asked, straightening his bow tie.

"She my *bambino*," Bartolomeo pressed out the wrinkles in his trousers. "I cry on Sunday, you see."

"Then you'll only have Sal in the house," Phil pointed out. "He's never leaving at this rate."

"No real broad wants that wet sock," Charlie joked about his youngest brother. "Not unless somebody slipped her a mickey." Thirty years earlier, Chicago saloon owner, Mickey Finn, notoriously drugged his rich patrons at his Dearborn Street bar, waited for them to pass out, and robbed them of money and jewelry. The crime earned the moniker slipping a mickey.

"You're nuts! A broad doesn't need alcohol to fall for me," Sal defended himself. "I think I look pretty smooth." He combed tonic into his coal-black hair.

"He'll be a dead hoofer on the dance floor," Phil added. He jabbed an elbow into Charlie's side.

"Enough!" Bartolomeo interrupted the brothers' heckling. He poked a wrinkled finger at his three sons. "You not ruin Faye's wedding day. She happy."

"Sorry, Pop," Sal, Phil, and Charlie replied.

The four men admired themselves in the mirror, all set for the wedding on Sunday.

A knock on the door interrupted them.

"I'll get it," Sal said, breaking the chain. Charlie and Phil left the room to change back into their daily clothes.

He opened the door to Paolo, the early summer sun casting a shadow on the front stoop. Paolo gripped a newspaper between his arm and side.

"Hi-ya, Sal," Paolo said. He nodded to his friend's excessive clothing for a Friday afternoon. "Oh, that's right, Faye's wedding is this weekend."

"Come on in," Sal directed. He held the front door open as Paolo squeezed past him.

Sal started untying his bow tie as Paolo headed toward Bartolomeo.

"*Buona sera, Signore* Scavuzzo," Paolo said. "You look swell. *Signora* Scavuzzo will want to make whoopee with you all night."

"Make whoopee?" Bartolomeo questioned. "What is make whoopee?"

"He's being funny, Pop," Sal explained. "I'll explain later."

"Enough with these clothes. We ready for Sunday. I make dinner soon. You go nowhere." Bartolomeo loosened his bow tie and headed toward the bedroom to change his clothes.

Out of earshot of his Pop, Sal nodded to the newspaper under Paolo's arm. "What's in there today? I haven't had a chance to read it."

"Capone was indicted for income tax fraud," Paolo said.

"What? Show me," Sal exclaimed.

Paolo pulled the paper out and laid it on top of the coffee table. The two friends hunched over it. "Right there." Paolo pointed to a headline that read:

Capone is Indicted in Income Tax Case

He read the secondary line, "Gangster surrenders and posts bail on charge of evading payment of $215,000." Below it displayed a picture of Al Capone in a white three-piece suit, with a smug look on his face.

Sal blew out a low whistle. "That's a lot of dough."

"Word on the street has him at having over a hundred million," Paolo added.

Paolo continued reading, "Scarface Alphonse Capone, number one among Chicago's public enemies, and reputedly the wealthiest of gangland leaders, surrendered to the government this afternoon and was released on $50,000 bail."

"Wow, Eddie was right," Sal noted. "He was afraid of something like this. I wonder if Eddie was indicted too?"

"I dunno," Paolo answered. "Best if you don't find out."

"This means Capone's getting locked up in the big house?" Sal begged the question.

"Sure seems like it," Paolo said. "Probably in a few months. You know it takes some time."

Sal exhaled deeply. With Al Capone going to jail, that meant he had little opportunity to put a hit out on Sal. Not with the coppers watching his every move. Sal still had to be careful until Capone was behind bars. He couldn't take any chances. He didn't know if Capone had henchmen on the ready to do jobs for him. Sal had already laid low for eight months since Joe Aiello was gunned down. He could wait it out for a few more.

Paolo spoke again, "But even with Capone in the big house, there are still a lot of gangsters in the city. Some are so quiet you don't even hear about 'em. They run the underground like rats."

Sal pondered the thought. With Capone heading to the clink and Aiello dead, that left Bugs Moran and the North Side Gang. But maybe someone else existed that he didn't know about? Whoever it was was off of Sal's radar. Regardless, he needed money.

"Did you get a chance to talk to Marco about a job for me?" Sal asked.

"Yeah, he said he has some small stuff for you," Paolo replied. "It'll get you a coupla five spots, but that's about it."

"I don't care," Sal said. "I'm down to my last nickels."

"Okay, I'll tell him you're in," Paolo said. "Enjoy Faye's wedding this weekend and I'll give you the low down on Monday."

"Thanks, pal," Sal replied. He nodded toward the kitchen where they could hear Sal's sisters and mother chatting about the wedding. "You staying for supper? My Pop's making arancini. Faye requested it."

Chapter 29

June 7, 1931

On the morning of Faye's wedding, Sal's siblings, parents, cousins, aunts, and uncles scurried in and out of the house making final preparations. Linens were spread on top of tables. Flowers were arranged. Hot food was pulled from ovens.

Faye was blessed with sun-filled skies for her wedding. Sal's baby sister chose June because she knew that most of her extended family took vacations in August and she didn't want to risk low attendance. The Scavuzzos never missed a wedding. Father Lazzeri had also warned her that marrying in August was believed to invite bad luck and sickness. Faye didn't want to take any chances. She kept to tradition by having the wedding on a Sunday, considered the luckiest day for the bond of matrimony.

Once Upon a Time in Chicago

With her infant son Michael swaddled against her bosom, Sal's older sister Rose chased after her eight-year-old son Raymond. She tried to keep the tyke's white shorts, dapper shirt, white socks, and matching patent leather shoes spotless. Raymond didn't want to be suited up and would have rather been playing in the street.

The house was filled with sweet aromas of roses and lilies for each of Faye's eight bridesmaids. Their sister Annie was charged with keeping the bouquets fresh and intact. Chattering and laughter of English and Italian buzzed around the home. The younger family members spoke in English, while the older relatives, and Theresa, conversed in Italian.

Following traditions, the night before, Theresa had gathered up hundreds of white candy-covered almonds in small mesh bags for the guests at her daughter's reception. The candies would help encourage conception for the happy couple. Sal knew how badly Faye wanted children. He could see them in his future too. His mother had also filled baskets full of paper confetti and rice. All of it would be thrown after the ceremony, wishing good fortune for Faye and Nicholas.

Dressed in his best suit, Sal found his younger sister in her room, standing in front of a tall mirror, nervously pressing out wrinkles in her wedding dress. Faye's dark hair was bound up into tight ringlets. Her headdress and veil of tiny roses with white ribbons lay on a padded chair next to her. Theresa knelt on the floor, checking the stitching on Faye's 12-foot silk train.

"You look *bellissima*, sis," Sal gushed. He hardly spoke Italian, as their Pop wanted them to learn English in his new country, but Sal felt it was appropriate for Faye's special day. He held her hand in his gloved hands and stepped closer to her. "You are lucky to have found Nicholas. You and he will have many great years together and many healthy children." He kissed her on both cheeks and stepped back to admire her. Her happiness filled him with joy.

"Thank you, Sal," Faye replied. Her cheeks blossomed into rosy rounds. "I feel so blessed."

A small pang of jealousy hit Sal. Faye was younger than him and getting married. He was the last of his siblings in the house. Would he be destined to live with his Pop and Ma for the rest of his life? He knew he wanted a wife eventually, but when would that be? Was it a twist of fate for his years of gambling, drinking, and chasing dames at the speakeasy?

Sal spoke again, "When you are all done in here, I'll escort you out to Pop. He and Charlie and Phil are almost ready. Charlie wants you and Pop to ride to the church in his car. That's part of his gift to you. And he is letting me drive it."

"That's wonderful!" Faye gushed, raising a gloved hand to her mouth. "Even with this long train, I had planned on walking the few blocks to Santa Maria." In the process, she shifted her whole body, causing her train to tear.

Their mother cursed something in Italian, straightened her back as she still knelt on the floor, and outstretched her arm, raising her palm upward. Theresa's face clouded with righteous indignation.

"Oh, Mama!" Faye bent down, to console her mother. "I'm so sorry I ripped it."

Theresa rattled something off in Italian and gestured back and forth to the ripped fabric.

"It'll be okay, Mama," Faye spoke in a soothing voice, placing her hands on Theresa's cheeks. "Just a few minutes to fix. I'm sorry."

Theresa spoke again in her native tongue, then finally stopped and grinned at her glowing daughter.

Sal smiled that his baby sister handled the mishap with grace and calm. He hadn't met a dame who would have dealt with it so well. Then he interrupted the mother and daughter tête-à-tête, "I'll tell Pop you'll be a few more minutes." He left the women to fix the train. He admired the resilience of his functional, working family that loved all of its members. He wanted that for himself. Eventually.

In the living room, Sal found his brothers and father lounging on the sofa, dressed in their finest. White roses were pinned to the left lapels of their black suits. Charlie and Phil had slicked their dark hair back with hair tonic. Each wore a black bow tie.

Bartolomeo puffed on a cigar, the smoke swirling into the air above his balding head.

"Make sure you put that away before Faye comes out, Pop," Sal warned with a pointed finger. "I'm sure she won't want to risk her gown catching fire after it got ripped already."

"I put out," Bartolomeo said to his youngest son, then took a drag. "You no worry."

Most of the other relatives had headed to the church. Annie wandered into the living room, carrying a bouquet and wearing a pink chiffon tea-length dress and matching hat. Soon, other matching bridesmaids wandered in carrying similar bouquets.

"We're ready," Annie spoke to her brothers and father. "Rose is on her way to the church with everyone else and Faye is almost done."

Charlie and Phil bolted from the couch and stood next to Sal. Taking his time, Bartolomeo snuffed out his cigar in a nearby ashtray and, placing a hand on his knee, angled himself off the sofa.

Sal's brothers escorted Annie and the bridesmaids out of the house, onto the sidewalk, and proceeded to the church.

The house was now empty, except for Sal, Faye, Bartolomeo, and Theresa.

A moment later, Faye and Theresa emerged into the living room. Sal and Bartolomeo gasped at Faye's beauty. Faye wore a long, white silk gown that barely touched the floor. Her 12-foot train took up space in the hallway behind her. A floral headdress and veil covered her angelic face. Her large bouquet of roses and lilies were draped with ribbons that almost touched the floor.

"*La mia bambina*," Bartolomeo gushed, wiping a tear from his eye. He embraced his youngest child and lifted her veil, kissing her on both cheeks.

Sal chuckled to himself that his Pop fell back into speaking all Italian.

"Are you ready?" Sal asked his sister. He checked his watch. "You don't want to keep your Nicholas waiting."

"Yes." An infectious smile spread across her face.

Sal ushered his family out the door, draping Faye's massive train in his arms so that it didn't snag again. He helped her to Charlie's car, a Buick Series 40, and held the door as she shimmied herself into the back seat. Bartolomeo assisted Theresa into the car next to Faye then sat in the front passenger side. Sal shut all of the doors then settled into the driver's seat.

A few minutes later, they arrived at Santa Maria's. Established in 1904, the burnt sienna brick church was built to serve the vibrant Italian-American community. Three massive oak double doors beckoned Sal, Faye, Bartolomeo, and Theresa into the wedding Mass. A large bowed ribbon was draped across the top of the middle doorway of the church, indicating to everyone who passed by that a marriage was about to take place inside. Above each door were multi-colored stained-glass windows depicting saints from the Bible. In the steeple, the bell tower heralded chimes throughout the neighborhood, signaling that the wedding was about to start.

Sal left his parents and sister in the vestibule and entered the main part of the church where his extended family and friends filled the pews. In contrast to the modern outside, the inside of the church reflected Renaissance styles of old Europe: the center nave with two side aisles, half a dozen glittering chandeliers suspended from the sweeping crisscrossed overhead arches, various statues of Christ and the Virgin Mary nestled inside sanctuary thrones.

Nicholas and his line of identically clothed attendants stood at the edge of the altar; his only distinguishable feature was a white bow tie while the other men wore black. Sal picked up his pace down the right aisle without drawing attention to himself and took his position at the end of the groomsman line. He loved being a part of his family dynamic.

The music started playing and Faye's bridesmaids bedecked in pink proceeded down the center nave.

An hour later, Faye and Nicholas were married, sealing the loving union with a kiss.

As the beaming couple was showered with rice and confetti on the outside steps, Sal couldn't help but smile that his little sister was happy. He was now the only child left in his parents' house. He was getting older and more single every day. If he wanted to change that, he needed to find a good woman--one he loved like how Nicholas loved Faye.

Chapter 30

The following week, Sal and Paolo strolled down Shields Avenue. The early summer weather brought out droves of kids playing in the streets now that school had concluded. A group of girls with bouncing hair skipped rope on the sidewalk, chanting rhyming songs. A few steps from them, another group of children held hands, sang, and danced around in a circle. Further up, boys huddled on the sidewalk concentrating on the marbles passing in front of them, betting with gum and pennies. Although the weather reached the high 70s, it wasn't warm enough to open up the fire hydrant so that the children could cool off. That was usually a July activity in the city.

Sal and Paolo hooked a right on West 26th Street, heading east.

"How was Faye's wedding last weekend?" Paolo asked as they stopped in front of some boys playing stickball in the street.

"Swell. She and Nicholas got hitched without a hitch. They're on their honeymoon in New York City now. They sent a telegram saying they are enjoying the sights. They collected enough money as gifts to take the trip."

"Good for them."

"Speaking of money, were you able to talk to Marco about any small jobs for me?" Sal pulled his trouser pockets inside out. "I'm outta dough."

Before Paolo could answer, a rogue ball rolled next to them. Sal picked up the tattered ball. He scanned the street and focused on a youth heading toward him wearing a half-untucked shirt and wrinkled shorts.

"Is this yours?" he asked the boy.

The boy nodded and Sal tossed the ball to him.

"Thanks, Mister!" the boy squealed and trotted off toward his playmates.

Sal turned back to Paolo.

"Yeah, he's got something if you're interested. Said it pays twenty a job," Paolo spoke in a low voice.

"I'm in," Sal remarked.

"You don't even want to know what you have to do first?" Paolo arched an eyebrow.

"Nah, I trust you." Sal shrugged.

"Well, I'm gonna tell you anyway," Paolo said, placing a hand on Sal's shoulder. "He needs a driver."

"Easy." Sal slapped his hands together.

"His regular driver is in the clink for three months because he was caught with over 500 frozen doves in his car on his way to Indiana. Fortunately, they weren't Marco's, so he's free and clear."

"Doves? As in the *bird*?" Sal pulled a cigarette pack out of his pocket and lit one. He offered one to Paolo. "Who has that many birds?"

Paolo smoked his cigarette and spoke out of the side of his mouth. "Yeah, the dumb S-O-B didn't know it was illegal to have more than 24 doves on you outside of hunting season. The G-Men caught him crossing state lines and threw him in the big house."

"I didn't know that either," Sal said. "What was he gonna do with that many birds?"

"I dunno," Paolo replied. "Train them to be stool pigeons?"

The friends howled in laughter.

"Anyway, Marco needs a driver for a few months," Paolo continued. "It could be anything from picking up people from the train station, delivering packages, or being the fake car for a copper tail. Nothing too dangerous."

"But I don't want to tell my Pop neither," Sal added.

"Exactly." Paolo took a long drag from his cigarette. "You still in?"

Sal didn't want to get in too deep with any illegal activities, but he also needed the money. All of the jobs that Paolo described seemed simple enough. It was only for a few months. Long enough to make some money, but short enough to easily back out if he felt he was in danger. He still worried that Capone could find him and have his goons toss him in Lake Michigan, but Sal's trust in Paolo outweighed that fear. They had been best friends for years. There wasn't much he didn't know about Paolo.

"Yeah, I'm in."

"Good, I'll let Marco know. When can you start?"

"Right away."

Sal and Paolo continued walking up West 26th Street. On the corner, a young boy in a newsboy cap was selling newspapers. "Get your Chicago news!" He pronounced Chicago like she-caw-go. A few customers huddled around him exchanging nickels for *The Chicago Daily News*.

"Hold on, I want to get one." Paolo nodded to the young entrepreneur.

He left Sal on the sidewalk to buy a newspaper, opening it up as he sauntered back.

"Listen to this." Paolo read the headline, "Al Capone pleads guilty of U.S. tax evasion, beer plotting. Sentence June 30th."

"Wow!" Sal cupped a hand to his mouth. "Who would've ever guessed that Capone would admit to that?" Sal was relieved that he could be out of Al Capone's line of fire.

"That can't be right." Paolo narrowed his eyes at the paper. He scanned the corresponding article. "It says he pled guilty to tax evasion and prohibition charges. Then he boasted that he struck a deal with the judge for a two-and-a-half-year sentence."

"That's nothin' for him," Sal interrupted, knowing that Capone could still hunt him down in two years. But a lot could happen in that time.

Paolo continued, "It says the presiding judge informed Capone that there was no such deal and that the judge was not bound to anything. Capone then changed his plea to not guilty."

"So, he's going to trial?"

"Seems like it," Paolo said as he read the rag. "In October."

"That still seems so far off," Sal sighed. The sooner that Al Capone went to jail, the better.

Chapter 31

August 1931

"This looks like the right place," Sal muttered to himself as he stopped in front of a glass storefront with a black awning. Above the awning, a sign for "Barden Furniture" swung slowly from its iron hinges. Next to Sal's unmarked delivery truck, several cars had parked in the diagonal slots against the sidewalk. A women's clothing boutique was to the right of the furniture store. To the left, on the corner, was Rosora's Cafe. The aroma of fresh bread spilled onto the sidewalk. Sal made a mental note to stop and get a slice there after his job.

He pulled a crumpled, small piece of paper from his pocket that Paolo had given him and read it. "Yep, Barden Furniture on Division

Street." With the back of his other hand, he wiped the summer humidity from his soaking forehead.

He needed to pick up a padded vanity bench from Mr. Barden for Marco. Easy money, Sal thought. If all of his jobs were this simple, he had no issues working for Marco. Even though he still hadn't met him. He had spent the last six weeks driving around the city like Paolo said. He had picked up a few travelers at the train station and dropped them off at the Congress Plaza Hotel. He had delivered a few small packages as well, receiving a ten spot in return. This job, however, promised twenty-five dollars. After he picked up the bench, he needed to deliver it to some joe named Harry at the docks.

Sal yanked one of the double wooden doors to Barden Furniture open and bells jingled in response. He entered the shop and his eyes went wide at the display of furniture before him. Wooden chairs were stacked on top of each other, almost reaching the ceiling. Several sofas were flipped inversely on one another, forming a narrow, jagged path to the back of the store. Porcelain vases and mirrors were stockpiled like children's toys in a well-used playroom. Despite all of the furniture, no human seemed to be in the store.

"Hello-oo," Sal called with a hand cupped at his mouth like a megaphone. "Anybody here?" His voice echoed into the depths of wood, iron, glass, and fabric.

"I'll be right out," a female voice called from the back.

Sal was pleasantly surprised by the gender of the voice since Paolo had told him to expect Mr. Barden to be there.

A few seconds later, a young woman appeared in front of Sal. Her curly brown hair was cut into a bob that fell just above the nape of her neck. She wore a blue and white striped, form-fitting top with matching blue wide-legged trousers that showed off her curvy hips.

Sal gaped at her chic and casual appearance. He was used to women in patterned dresses and hats. She was cute, despite her unexpected appearance.

"Can I help you?" she asked, wiping her hands on a rag that she pulled from her back pocket.

"Uh, yes," Sal managed to say, still taken in by her beauty. "I'm here to see Mr. Barden."

"He's not here," the young woman replied.

"I can wait until he comes back." Sal surely didn't think that this woman, as attractive as she was, could lift a vanity bench. Especially if it was underneath a mountain of furniture.

"He won't be back until tomorrow," the woman said. "I can help you."

Sal chuckled to himself. "Not unless a doll like you can lift a big piece of furniture."

She scoffed, pocketed the rag, and planted her hands on her hips. "Listen Mr. Know-It-All, I'm plenty rugged to move furniture around."

Sal was taken aback by her unprecedented attitude. All of the other dames he had ever encountered were meek and demure. Not confident. And sexy.

"Okay then," Sal said, "I'm here to pick up a vanity bench."

The young woman glared at him, arching a brow. "What kind of vanity bench? We have dozens."

"Uh... I ... don't know." Sal was never told the details of what the bench looked like. Paolo said Marco told Sal to pick it up. Sal assumed that Mr. Barden would know what he was talking about.

The attractive woman glared at Sal, waiting on an answer. Her almond-shaped eyes bore into him. He found it hard to concentrate on anything else.

"Marco... he said... to pick up--" Sal started to say as he spoke with his hands.

"Marco?" the young woman piped up. "Why didn't you say so! Follow me." She turned on her heels and entered the labyrinth of stacked furniture behind her. Sal didn't want to lose her in the furniture maze and hurried to keep up with her. He couldn't keep his eyes off her cute curves.

She stopped at the far wall of the shop, near the loading doors that opened into the back alley. "This is it." She pointed to an art deco mahogany and maple bench that had been recently upholstered with new gold and black patterned fabric.

Sal bent down to pick it up but stopped when the young woman stepped in front of him.

"What do you think you're doing?" she spoke. "I just told you that I can move furniture. Did you not hear anything through your thick head?"

"But--" Sal started to say. Her hot tongue could slice through a block of ice.

"You lug-heads think you know everything about women."

Sal had met his match. And liked her more with every word she spoke.

"Very well." Sal stepped aside and raised his hand in a go-ahead motion.

The young woman elbowed her way past him and lifted the bench into her arms. She grunted a few times as her grip slipped, but she recovered and marched toward the front of the shop. Sal followed behind.

As they approached the front door, Sal ran ahead and held the door open for her.

She stopped on the sidewalk and lowered the vanity bench to the cement.

"This is as far as I go," she said. "You're on your own the rest of the way."

Sal rocked back on his heels, admiring her for a moment. "No problem. I can take it from here."

He glanced over at his truck and back at the attractive brunette in front of him. If he had a different car, he would have taken her out on a date after she was done working.

"Thank you," Sal said.

"You're welcome."

"What's your name, anyway?"

"Betsy," she said, offering her hand. "Betsy Barden."

"You're the boss's daughter?" Sal asked, more of a statement than a question as he shook her hand.

Betsy nodded with a proud grin. "Yes, I am."

He checked her left hand for a ring. It was bare, but he hoped she wasn't like Mae. "Any chance that Miss Barden would like to go out for lunch sometime? I turn 22 next week. Why don't you help me celebrate?" Sal hoped that she would want to see him again as much as he wanted to see her.

"You work for Marco, right?" Betsy avoided the question.

"Yeah, why?"

"Sorry, but I don't mix business with pleasure." Betsy headed back into the shop, leaving Sal alone with the vanity bench on the sidewalk.

Sal was dumbfounded. Was he losing his touch with the ladies? First Dottie, now Betsy. He hadn't gained 50 pounds or lost his hair. What was it that made them turn him down? It had been a while since he was at the speakeasy where the dames were so easy to catch that they practically threw themselves at him. They were like shooting fish in a barrel. Maybe he needed to go back to gain some confidence? But was he willing to risk going back into the underworld where Al Capone and his goons could still find him? His nightmares had lessened, but he still couldn't take any chances.

Chapter 32

Twenty minutes later, Sal parked the delivery truck along Wacker Drive, a half block from the river docks. Sal hopped out of the truck and unloaded the vanity bench onto the sidewalk. He scooped it up in his arms and headed toward the iron staircase that led from street level to the landing. At the bottom of the stairs, hordes of sweaty men unloaded cargo from boats and loaded them onto nearby palettes, ready to be lifted upward to awaiting trucks. Wavy plumes of white smoke filled the air as boats grunted along the Chicago River, waiting to port.

Paolo had told Sal to meet Harry at the big sign for Goodrich Docks at 2:00. A few minutes early, Sal hoisted the bench over his shoulder and headed toward the black and white sign. As a man in grey overalls pushed a cart of filled burlap sacks, Sal wished he had something with which to carry the bench. It was easy to lift at first, but the weight seemed heavier and heavier in the summer afternoon heat. His arms ached and he didn't envy the bodily pains the men around him faced every day. Some of them looked and smelled like they hadn't bathed in weeks.

In twenty more steps, Sal reached the Goodrich sign. Even though dozens of workers were milling about, no one stopped what they were doing to notice Sal. He set the bench on the cement and studied his surroundings. He wasn't sure what Harry looked like but hoped he didn't have to wait long for him.

Several minutes went by as men hauled sacks over their shoulders and loaded carts of large boxes. Sal hoped he was in the right place. He checked his watch and it read 2:10. Harry was late. Sal didn't want to wait around much longer, especially in an unfamiliar seedy place.

Just as he was about to load the bench back on his shoulder and head home, a man in stained grey overalls and a matching tattered cap stopped him with a raised pointed finger.

"You Sal?" the man asked. His cheeks were covered in soot.

"Yeah. Are you Harry?"

"No. Follow me," the man replied.

Sal grunted as he lifted the bench onto his shoulders again, annoyed that the curt man didn't offer to help. He followed the man through a maze of workers, carts, and pallets, ducking under wires and small cranes.

The man finally came to a stop near a utility building, where dockworkers were smoking and waiting for their next delivery. He led Sal into the building through a screen door that slammed on tight springs behind them.

Inside, Sal came face to face with a large man standing behind a wooden desk, a cigar perched from his lips. The large man nodded to the one who led Sal there and that man exited, without saying a word. Sal assumed that the large man was Harry. Sal still carried the bench on his shoulder, unsure if he should set it down.

"Put it down here." Harry directed to a cleared space in the tight room. Crates and barrels stacked on top of each other filled the perimeter.

Sal did what he was told, relieved to be rid of the extra weight.

"Have any problems?" Harry inquired.

"Not at all." Sal shook his head but wanted to add *only with the boss's daughter*. The encounter with Betsy still wandered through his mind.

Harry walked around to the front of the desk and inspected the vanity bench. Kneeling down, he ran his fingers along the carved edges and smooth gold and black fabric. He slowly ran his hand on the underneath of the bench and smiled at Sal.

"This'll do." Harry puffed on his cigar and exhaled. A billow of smoke filled the air above his head.

Sal wondered what prompted the passing inspection but was afraid to ask. He had learned from Paolo and when working for Eddie that sometimes it was better if he didn't know.

"Tell Marco that everything looks good," Harry said, as he rose to his feet. "And that I'll need another shipment in a few weeks."

"Will do," Sal said. He glanced around the small office, unsure what he should do next.

"That'll be all, kid." Harry waved dismissively at Sal. He walked back around to his desk and sat down. The wooden chair protested under his large body as he started reviewing a stack of order slips that he pulled from a drawer.

Sal took heed to Harry's abruptness and headed out the door. The unexpected gruffness still took some getting used to, but Sal wouldn't ask questions that might land him in hot water. Sal wove his way back through the maze of dockworkers and found the stairs that led back to Wacker Drive.

* * * *

After he parked the empty truck in an almost vacant lot around the corner from Shields Avenue, Sal wandered down the sidewalk to find Paolo to collect his cash. Paolo was sitting on the stoop of his flat, smoking a cigarette.

"We gotta be quiet," Paolo whispered. "My Ma's sleeping in the front room." The two-story brick rowhouse windows were open to allow the summer breeze to flow in.

"Okay." Sal sat on the stoop next to his friend.

"Want one?" Paolo pulled the cigarette out of his mouth and gestured it toward Sal.

"Yeah."

Paolo reached into his pocket and grabbed his pack of cigarettes, pinched one out, and handed it to Sal. Sal squeezed it between his fingers and held it to his lips as Paolo lit it.

"How did everything go today?" Paolo wanted to know.

"Fine."

"You run into any problems?"

"I struck out again with a dame, but other than that, no," Sal said.

Paolo chuckled, "Ol' Man Barden's daughter?"

"Yep. Betsy." Sal took a drag on his cigarette. "Said she didn't mix business with pleasure."

"She's said that to me a few times too," Paolo added. "Don't worry about it. There are plenty of other sweet mamas in this city."

Sal knew that was true, even though he was striking out like Babe Ruth when the Sultan of Swat wasn't hitting homers. He hoped his dry streak would end.

"You have dough for me?" Sal asked.

Paolo reached into his pocket and handed Sal a small stack of Lincolns. "Here ya go, pal. Paid in full."

Sal stuffed the money into his pocket. "You ever ask your cousin what he really does?"

"He's in furniture sales," Paolo laughed. "But no, Marco don't talk details with me. Says the less I know, the better. Do you care if you don't know?"

"I guess not." Sal shrugged. He didn't always know what Eddie was doing, so what difference did it make who paid him now.

"You still want the small jobs though?" Paolo asked.

"Yeah, I need the cash. Times are tight," Sal sighed. "I might not be able to afford a new car, but at least I can get breakfast out with you at Lou Mitchell's. Wanna go next week and see Thea?"

Chapter 33

October 17, 1931

"It's been a week, but I still can't believe the Cards won the World Series in the seventh game!" Sal slapped a hand down on the counter at Lou Mitchell's. "I brought in some cash!"

"You lucky duck." Paolo lightly jabbed his friend in the rib. The friends had been nursing cups of coffee for the past half hour. "No one had a clue who would win. Not after the Athletics tied up the series in game six."

Sal downed his last remaining drops with a gulp.

"I thought you gave up gambling?" Thea interrupted them with a full carafe of hot coffee.

"Only the dice and the cards," Sal said. He nodded to her steaming pot in an unspoken motion to fill him up. "This one was on baseball. And I had a gut feeling to not pick the two-time defending champs. The Cards' win brought me twenty-five big ones!"

Paolo shook his head at his friend. "I can't believe I bet on the Athletics. I shoulda gone with you."

"What plans do you have with your winnings?" Thea asked, setting the coffee pot on the counter.

"I dunno," Sal said. "Maybe buy me a new leather jacket at Marshall Fields. I haven't decided."

"Maybe you could add some of the dough to my tip?" Thea jested.

"Don't worry, Thea," Sal replied with a sly grin. "I always take care of you."

"Because if you didn't, your Ma and Pop would hear about it," she warned. "Your Ma might not speak English, but she knows what I say to her."

"Your Ma might put a curse on you." Paolo pointed to Sal.

Before Sal could defend himself, the bell jingled on the front door and a street peddler rushed in and stood in the doorway. He panted as his apron flapped in the breeze. Most of the people in the diner stared up at the man.

"Did you hear the news?" he blurted. His eyes were wide as he yanked a folded newspaper from his back pocket and spread it open so that everyone could see the front page. "Capone is guilty. He's going to the big house!"

Once Upon a Time in Chicago

On his *Chicago Sunday Tribune*, in bold fat letters, the headline read:

Al Capone Guilty of Tax Evasion

Excited, the man hustled toward Sal and Paolo. He settled on a nearby stool, catching his breath from the scandalous news. He slapped the newspaper flat on the counter, pushing it in Sal's direction.

"Can I see that?" Sal asked.

"Sure, pal," the man replied, still a little out of breath.

"Thanks, buddy," Sal said. He turned to Thea and said, "Can you get him a cup? It's on me."

Thea nodded in response to Sal's offer and poured the man a cup of coffee.

Sal slid the newspaper toward him and Paolo and read the rest of the headline. "Owed over $215,000 in back taxes."

Paolo blew out a low whistle. "That's a lot of dough to owe the Feds."

Sal continued reading, "Sentenced to 11 years in prison." He pointed to a snapshot of Al Capone dressed in a white fedora with black satin trim and a three-piece suit. Capone crossed his hands one over the other and had a smug look on his face. His dark eyebrows formed an arrogant unibrow across his face. "That guy doesn't seem like he's heading to the clink."

"More like he's having fun at a speakeasy to see Bing Crosby sing," Paolo added.

"I heard he boasted that the Feds couldn't collect legal taxes from illegal money," Thea said.

"Guess it finally caught up with him," the street peddler replied.

Sal exhaled deeply at the city's popular headline. A year had gone by since Joe Aiello was killed and Sal had spent most of it laying low. He had done a few jobs for Paolo's cousin but they were just enough to bring him a few dollars; not enough to save for anything. Once, when his Ma sent him to the grocer, a group of men in long trench coats paraded down the street, raising Tommy Guns in the air. In a panic, Sal had darted into the store and hid behind some boxes. Sal later learned that the gangsters weren't hunting him, but the fear haunted him.

This news about Capone brought on colossal relief. Sal no longer had to worry that Capone would send his goons after him and shoot him down in the middle of the street. Capone had a reputation to show no mercy when it came to snitches and snakes. Sal could now walk freely and not purposely dress so that he blended in with a crowd.

Sal could even go to a speakeasy now if he wanted. He hadn't played cards or bet on dice in a long time. He missed the excitement, the exhilaration of winning, the fun. He also missed the dames. Boy, did he miss the dames. He longed for the dolls to hang on his every word and laugh at his silly jokes. He needed that ego boost again. Especially since Dottie and Betsy had turned him down.

Folding up the newspaper, Sal handed it back to its original owner. "Thanks, pal," he said to the man.

Sal turned to Paolo again. "What'dya say we go to the speakeasy tomorrow night?"

"You haven't been there in ages. I thought you'd never ask!" Paolo smiled wide.

* * * *

The following night, Sal admired himself in his full-length mirror. Freshly shaved, he slapped some aftershave on his cheek and combed tonic through his hair until it shined like gleaming asphalt in the middle of July. He wore a double-breasted, dark brown three-piece suit in a windowpane pattern. The broad-shouldered jacket added the illusion of height and width and the wide-leg trousers sat high on Sal's waist. Cuffed pants grazed the top of his newly shined shoes. Knife-creased trousers completed the look. Except for Faye's wedding four months earlier, Sal couldn't remember the last time he wore his Sunday best.

He stuffed a clean handkerchief into his breast pocket, popped on a black fedora, pocketed his billfold, and headed out the door to meet Paolo.

Fifteen minutes later, the burly bouncer admitted Sal into the South Halsted Street speakeasy. He walked with a confident gait, his heels barely clicking on the wooden floor.

In the main room, Sal breathed in his surroundings with a broad smile. Many couples foxtrotted and lindied in front of a nine-piece band playing trumpets, trombones, and a rhythm section. A handful of waitresses wandered the area wearing low-cut dresses to show off their full bosoms as they hawked cigarettes and shots of hooch. Crowds of people in their prim suits and dresses lined the bar, downing drinks and sharing stories. Jocularity, music, and booze filled the atmosphere.

Sal spotted Paolo at the far corner of the bar and Paolo waved him over. As Sal sauntered over toward Paolo, he caught the eye of several beautiful dames along his path. Blondes. Brunettes. Redheads. They all smelled like vanilla and smiled wantonly at him. From their head-to-toe gazes and obvious bites on their bottom lips, they put a pep in his step.

Sal grabbed the barstool next to his friend. "I missed this place!"

Paolo nodded toward the crowd. "I think those sweet mamas missed you too. I saw them eyeing you up."

Sal retrieved a cigarette out of his pocket and lit it. He tipped his head back toward the beautiful women. "Yeah, I'm a little rusty, but I'm sure my way with the broads'll come back to me. Just like riding a bike."

"You'll be ridin' something soon, that's for sure," Paolo chuckled.

Sal and Paolo spent the next few hours downing whiskey, delightfully dancing with different women, and enjoying a night out on the town. At the end of the night, Sal left the speakeasy with a pocketful of napkins that the women had written their names and phone numbers on. Those napkins were worth more than money.

Chapter 34

February 27, 1932

Another winter storm covered Chicago. Pure snow covered rooftops, devoid of any disruption. Tainted snow on the sidewalks and streets constantly fought against cars and pedestrians ruining its unadulterated shine. Like Sal, many of the city's residents wished they were somewhere south and warm.

Wind whipped between buildings, driving against men holding onto their hats. Women tried in vain to keep their long skirts from showing any forbidden skin. Doors banged and discarded boxes traveled through empty alleys like tumbleweeds. The winter storm wanted nothing more than to say, "I'm still here. You haven't escaped me yet."

In his parents' warm house, Sal perched on the sofa in the front room. He yanked on his boots, tightening the laces against the black leather.

"Where you going?" Bartolomeo gestured toward the snow collecting on the windowpane. "No time to be out."

"Don't worry, Pop," Sal comforted him. "I have to pick up something with Paolo, then I'll be right back."

"What Paolo have you doing?" Bartolomeo held his palm up toward his son. "Weather is bad."

"Just getting a parlour couch." Sal gathered his overcoat and hat from the coat rack. "We need to deliver it to the furniture store." Sal didn't want to tell his Pop that he was meeting Paolo at the docks first and hoped he would be satisfied with Sal's answer. He was sure that his Pop wouldn't approve.

"What furniture store?" Bartolomeo narrowed his eyes at his youngest son.

Sal wasn't sure; Paolo would tell him once he arrived at the docks. He had to think fast to appease his Pop, otherwise, he could be an unwilling victim of a Sicilian curse. "Barden's on Division."

"Jack Barden?"

"I think so," Sal fibbed. In reality, Sal had no idea. He never learned Betsy's father's first name.

"He good man." Bartolomeo's features softened into a warm smile. "He get me washing machine. Your Mama use it all time." Sal remembered installing it and how his Pop had saved enough cash to purchase it.

"I gotta head out, Pop," Sal changed the subject and stepped toward the door. He buttoned his jacket and placed a hat on his head.

"Jack has *bella* daughter," Bartolomeo mused. "You meet her. You get married like Faye. Find nice girl." He accompanied Sal to the front door.

"Maybe someday, Pop."

Closing the door behind him, Sal stepped outside and onto the front stoop. His Pop was right; Jack Barden did have a beautiful daughter, but Betsy wanted nothing to do with him. That was okay for now because Sal had plenty of dames at his disposal at the speakeasy. He had been enjoying socializing at the speakeasy for the past few months, much to the chagrin of his Pop's persistence to get married. He'd met Ruth, Elizabeth, Mabel, Beverly, Peggy, and Louise. Those were the ones whose names Sal remembered. There were plenty more women whom he couldn't place but still enjoyed their company at the speakeasy. Their carefree lifestyle and attention helped him forget about Dottie, Betsy, and Mae. Sal didn't bother asking the dames from the club if they went to college or held jobs, because he didn't care.

As Sal pushed against the wind on Shields Avenue, he folded his jacket collar up against his neck. His eyes watered and all but froze in their sockets. A few cars rolled by, spattering slushy snow against the sidewalk. Several other people braved the wind as well, diving for cover in nearby restaurants and shops.

Sal hopped the trolley and disembarked at Wacker Drive. City workers had set fire to the nearby train tracks to make sure the L kept humming. Vibrant flames rose from coal-fed heaters that ran alongside the rails and kept them warm.

Paolo had planned to meet Sal on Wacker with the truck after he made other deliveries. This job would earn Sal thirty dollars--enough dough to join a future card game. Sal had played a few rounds with Paolo and the boys but kept to conservative bets. He didn't want to have to borrow money again like he had with Joe Aiello.

At the docks, Sal stopped at the bottom of the iron staircase. He didn't want to get lost in the crowd of dockworkers transferring cargo waiting to be lifted by crane to the sidewalk above.

"What're you doing here?" a gruff voice bellowed from the milling bunch of men.

Sal was unsure of the voice's owner and disregarded it, assuming that it was meant for someone else.

"I said what're you doing here?" the voice hollered again.

Sal was startled by an ogre of a man in front of him. The man's face was covered with half a dozen scars that ran the length of both cheeks and across his forehead. He wore a tattered newsboy cap that barely covered his gargantuan head. The overcoat he wore bore various rips and stains.

Sal swallowed hard, unsure what to do. He could run off, but then he was afraid he'd miss Paolo.

"What're you starin' at, kid?" the man demanded. In one step of his clunky boots, he closed any remaining social space between him and Sal.

Sal was too stunned to reply.

"You deaf or somethin'? You twit." The man grabbed the front of Sal's jacket, scrunching it in his massive hand and knocking Sal's hat to the ground. He raised his other arm in a heavy fist, drawing back in Sal's line of sight.

Sal still couldn't get words to come out of his mouth, tensing himself to be pummeled. He knew dockworkers had a reputation to have short fuses but didn't understand why he was the target. His eyes clamped shut, preparing to be knocked to the ground.

"Stop!" Another voice called. Sal shot his eyes open.

The beast of a man lowered his fist and let go of Sal's jacket. Paolo approached the wannabe prizefighter.

Sal sighed heavily, as his shoulders relaxed.

"Thank God," Sal whispered, finally finding his voice.

"This is my pal, Sal," Paolo said to the large man. "What do you think you're doing?"

"I didn't know," the man said, his voice barely audible.

"Leave him alone." Paolo narrowed his eyes at the leviathan. "*Capisce?*"

"Yes, sir."

Sal couldn't believe the man's quick change from brute to a meek field mouse. The man ran off, disappearing into the crowd of dockworkers.

"What just happened there?" Sal smoothed out his jacket, making sure he was presentable again. He bent down and picked up his hat, slapping slush from it, before placing it back on his head. "That greaseball almost walloped me."

"Maybe he didn't like the way you looked?"

"But you stopped him." Sal arched an eyebrow at his friend.

"I guess he knew I was Marco's cousin." Paolo shrugged.

"Marco must have a big goon squad to scare the shit out of people," Sal wondered. "I still haven't met this cousin of yours."

"Not many people have," Paolo said. "He likes to keep things on the Q.T. Says his quiet reputation is his greatest asset."

"Sounds like a smart joe," Sal replied.

"Speaking of other smart joes," Paolo added, "or maybe not-so-smart joes. Did you hear that Capone lost his appeal for his tax fraud conviction?"

"Nah, I didn't," Sal said. "So, he's staying in the clink for a while?"

"Yeah, it was in the paper today."

Sal blew out a relieved sigh. The more time Capone spent in jail, the better chance Sal had that Capone wouldn't think he was a snitch.

"Let's go get that parlour couch." Paolo motioned for Sal to follow him.

The friends wove through the labyrinth of dockworkers and headed toward Harry's humble office. Harry had the couch ready for them, wrapped in a blanket to protect it from the snow. They each took an end of the couch and carried it back along the dock, passing other men hauling crates and barrels. They lifted it up the iron staircase and loaded it into Paolo's waiting truck.

Chapter 35

May 8, 1932

"Thank you, Mister Barden," Sal said to the furniture store owner who stood before him. "I'll make sure this is delivered with care."

A wooden desk with brass handles and intricately carved legs rested on the cement between them in front of Barden Furniture. As his daughter Betsy did before, Jack Barden's assistance ended at the edge of his sidewalk.

Sal admired the handiwork on the desk. The pattern and markings resembled a python. "What kind of wood is that? It's not like anything I've seen before."

"It's Snakewood," Barden explained. "Whoever is getting this desk is getting one of the most expensive woods in the world. Had to special order it." Jack hooked his fingers into the belt loops of his pants in pride.

"I dunno. Maybe President Hoover?" Sal chuckled.

"I'll see you again in a few weeks," Barden said. "Sorry you missed Betsy today. Maybe next time."

Despite Sal's ongoing requests to join him for a meal, Betsy continued to turn him down. He assumed she told her father about it. Maybe they laughed at Sal's expense?

"See ya 'round, Mister Barden."

Barden entered his store, as bells on the door jingled behind him. Sal had been coming to the store several times a month for the past nine months picking up different items--a chaise, a sofa, a bed, and one time an entire dining room set. He, and sometimes Paolo, would deliver the furniture to Harry on the docks, or bring it back to Jack. Sal earned anywhere from fifteen to forty dollars a job, depending on the item. Betsy or Jack always assisted Sal inside their shop but never helped him load the item into his truck.

Bending down, Sal wrapped his arms around the enormous desk. He grunted as he tried to lift it but it barely budged. It was as if the desk was cemented to the sidewalk. He didn't remember it being this heavy when he helped Jack carry it from inside the store. Even though Jack had several grey hairs on his head, he didn't struggle like an old man when they moved the desk. What Sal wouldn't give for a wheeled cart right now.

Sal weighed his options for assistance on the street around him. A few patrons were entering nearby Rosora's Cafe. Cars rumbled down the street, blasting puffs of exhaust behind them. A young woman in a spring dress clutched the hand of a small boy in fancy knickers as they hurried down the block. Sal surmised that they wouldn't do.

"You look like you could use some help," a male voice startled Sal from his investigative thoughts. A man in a white linen suit and matching boater hat approached him and pointed to the unforgiving desk.

"What-- Yeah," Sal stuttered, gathering his words. In a city of 3.5 million, he was thankful for the lone man's generosity. "That'd be awfully kind of you, sir."

"My pleasure."

Together, Sal and the man lifted the heavy desk and loaded it into Sal's empty truck. Back at the sidewalk, Sal offered his hand to the man. "Thank you, sir."

"Anytime." The kind man shook Sal's hand. "Anytime you need some assistance around here, you look me up."

"What's your name?"

"Michael Russo. How about you?"

"Sal Scavuzzo."

"Pleasure to meet you, Sal," Michael said. "My wife and I just moved in up the street. She and I had a baby a few months ago. My first son." His eyes gleamed as he talked proudly of his child.

"Congratulations."

The man nodded toward an opening door at the nearby women's boutique. Sal followed his gaze. A woman under a large-brimmed hat pushed a baby carriage onto the sidewalk next to them.

"Here they are now." Michael waved the woman closer to him. Their baby napped silently in his carriage.

"Honey," Michael said to his wife, "I'd like you to meet Sal."

As Michael's wife lifted her chin to greet them, Sal came face to face with Mae. His jaw dropped and he stifled his surprise. Russo was a common name so Sal didn't think twice when Michael said his last name moments earlier. Sal hadn't seen Mae since he jumped out of her second-story window when her husband came home unexpectedly. Her husband Michael. Sal never saw Michael's face that fateful day two years earlier. He swallowed hard, hoping Michael didn't still own a gun.

Mae offered a gloved hand to Sal, her eyes boring into him, pleading with him not to reveal their secret tryst. "Nice to meet you, Sal. I'm Mae."

"Hello, Mae." Sal turned his head away from Michael's line of sight and winked at Mae so that only she could see his eyes. They locked eyes for a moment, neither speaking.

Sal didn't want an altercation on the public street with Michael, but he didn't want Mae to think he forgot about her either. Even two years later, she held a special place in his heart. He tried to forget her with other women and whiskey but seeing her now brought him back to spending hours in her bed. He knew he could never have her again, but that didn't erase the feelings.

He gazed toward the sleeping baby in its carriage. The infant appeared to be three months old. Sal exhaled quietly, confident that the little boy could not have been his.

Michael spoke to his wife, interrupting Sal's thoughts, "I told Sal to look me up if he ever needs some help around here."

"That's kind of you, honey," Mae replied. She bent down, conveniently adjusting the light blanket over her sleeping son.

Sal wondered if she did that to avoid eye contact with him.

"We need to move along," Michael said, corralling his wife. "Take care of yourself, Sal." He offered his hand to Sal.

"Will do." Sal shook Michael's hand but doubted he'd take him up on his offer. He couldn't face the man again whose wife he made whoopee with. This encounter on the sidewalk was serendipitous, but Sal didn't want to orchestrate another one.

Fifteen minutes later, Sal parked the delivery truck at the curb in front of Lou Mitchell's. He planned to meet Paolo inside to get a bite to eat and get paid for picking up the desk.

Sal locked the truck and pushed the glass doors open into the diner. He spotted Paolo at the counter and headed toward him.

"Everything go okay?" Paolo asked as Sal settled in a stool next to him. In front of Paolo was a half-empty cup of coffee and the current copy of the *Chicago Tribune*.

"Yeah, the desk is in the truck," Sal said. He waved a finger to Thea. She was at the other end of the counter taking care of another customer. "But let me tell you, that thing was heavier than a barrel of bourbon."

Paolo laughed out loud, nearly knocking his cup of coffee over.

Thea came by and poured a cup for Sal. She flashed the friends a brief smile, then wandered off to take care of another customer in the busy diner.

"Some guy on the street offered to help me load it in the truck," Sal continued. "You'll never guess who he was." He sipped his steaming coffee.

"Who?"

"Mae's husband."

"Mae who? Mae from the club, Mae?" Paolo leaned closer to Sal. "I didn't know she was married."

Sal scoffed. "Me either. She has a baby too." Sal still couldn't bring himself to tell his best friend that he knew Mae was married two years earlier.

"Guess that's why we haven't seen her at the speakeasy lately."

"Not unless they're allowing babies on the dance floor any time soon." Sal slapped a hand on the counter, laughing at his joke.

He nodded toward Paolo's newspaper. "Anything good in there today?"

"Not much." Paolo pointed to a couple of headlines. "The president of France was assassinated... and Capone made it to the Atlanta prison. Says he's enjoying cigars and a set of encyclopedias."

"Doesn't sound like prison to me," Sal muttered.

"I bet soon enough he gets broads in there too," Paolo laughed.

Thea came by, interrupting them. "Sorry I couldn't chat earlier. It's been busy. What can I get you boys to eat?" She leaned against the counter in front of them, the buttons on her white uniform dress puckering at the pressure.

"Just a club sandwich for me," Sal said.

"I'll have the same," Paolo replied.

"Coming right up," Thea said. She headed toward the grill where William Mitchell was sizzling bacon on the griddle.

"Before I forget," Paolo stated, "I owe you this." He reached into his pocket, pulled a crumpled bill out, and handed it to Sal.

Sal unfolded it to see a picture of Ulysses Grant on the money.

Sal blew out a low whistle. "Whoa. This is a lot more than what I usually bring in."

"Yeah, I know," Paolo explained. "Marco said you've been doing a lot for him lately and he wanted to give you a little extra this time."

Sal smiled, his teeth taking over most of his face. "Tell your cousin that I'm happy to work for him. Too bad he can't help me out with Betsy Barden."

Chapter 36

July 1932

The city of Chicago was bustling despite being an epicenter for the Great Depression. As lines for food banks stretched blocks, big names from Washington descended upon the city for three weeks for the Democratic and Republican nominating conventions. The upcoming election would be the most crucial in American history. President Hoover had hoped to win again while New York Governor Franklin Roosevelt vied to upset him.

When Sal wanted a break from the political discourse, he tuned in to his radio to hear about the Summer Olympics in Los Angeles. American favorite, Babe Didrikson, won gold for javelin and hurdles.

Once Upon a Time in Chicago

Sal enjoyed being outside during Chicago summers. He watched as children played under an open fire hydrant. The spray of water mixed with sunshine created a misty rainbow banner. Street peddlers carrying fresh apples and tomatoes tipped their hats at him as he sauntered by.

On his way to meet Paolo at Lou Mitchell's a couple of blocks away, Sal stopped for a break in the traffic at the corner of Jackson Boulevard and South Wacker Drive. A newsboy shouting the headlines of the *Tribune* caught his attention.

"Cubbies win 75 games! World Series bound!" the young lad hollered to anyone who wanted to buy his rag.

Sal knew the World Series was three months off, but he admired the kid's confidence in their hometown team.

He exchanged a nickel for the newspaper and opened it up. He read the headlines about the Cubs, the political conventions, and the Olympics.

One small article at the bottom of the first page caught his eye. The headline read:

Bugs Moran Held for Quiz in Gang Slaying

Sal knew that Bugs Moran, head of the North Side Gang and a rival of Al Capone, was the last major gangster in the city. He insisted he was merely a country gentleman hoping to retire. Moran was arrested for the machine gun slaying of George Barker, an ambitious henchman in the Capone organization.

Even with Capone locked up in Atlanta, gang killings had resumed in the city in recent weeks. Sal assumed Bugs Moran was behind it all, even though he had been out of the limelight. But were there more? Paolo had always told Sal that criminals lurked in the shadows, and Sal wondered who now controlled the city's underground.

"Hey Mister, you got a smoke?" the newsboy interrupted Sal as he read the rest of the paper on the sidewalk.

"What--" Sal faced the boy, who sported a trio of hairs on his chin. "Aren't you too young to smoke, kid?"

"No way." The boy stood up a little taller, showing off his maturity. "I've been smoking for three years now."

"You're on your own." Even though Sal had a pack of cigarettes in his pocket, he wasn't giving one to a kid.

The boy made an obscene gesture toward Sal and moved on to his next customer.

Sal folded up his newspaper, shoved it in his back pocket, and headed off to meet Paolo. A handful of cars and trucks motored down the street. The sidewalks were relatively empty, unusual for a summer afternoon. Sal wondered where everyone was. Maybe they were bathing on the beaches of Lake Michigan.

Sal spotted Paolo standing in front of Lou Mitchell's, a half block away. Paolo was reviewing a small notebook in his hand and didn't notice Sal. Paolo wore a white shirt, black suspenders, and black trousers, comfortable for the summer.

As Sal stepped off the sidewalk to cross the street, a black Ford Model B careened down the blacktop, causing Sal to jump backward. He stumbled and fell to the sidewalk. As he found his bearings, he caught a glimpse of the long black barrel of a Tommy Gun pointed toward Paolo.

"Paolo!" Sal ran off down the street toward his friend. "Paolo! Watch out!" Sal waved his hands frantically above his head in hopes to catch Paolo's attention.

RAT-A-TAT-TAT! RAT-A-TAT-TAT!

The sound of gunfire consumed the scene.

The Model B sped off down the street and Sal ran a few steps after it, trying to figure out who was inside. Stopping and out of breath, he gave up as the car disappeared into traffic on the next block.

"You okay, Paolo?" Sal spoke toward his friend but still focused on the empty street.

Paolo groaned in response.

Sal turned toward the sidewalk and found Paolo lying on the cement. Blood veined across his once-white shirt and he held a bloody hand to his chest. More blood seeped from his mouth.

Sal ran over and crouched next to Paolo. He held his friend's hand and frantically searched for the source of the wound.

"Help! Somebody help!" Sal screamed. A few people came outside from Lou Mitchell's but Sal wasn't sure if anyone was calling the ambulance. He cradled Paolo in his arms.

"Sal... Sal..." Paolo gasped. He slowly and blindly searched for the sidewalk with his hand.

"It'll be okay, Paolo. Don't try to get up." Sal squeezed his friend's hand. "It'll be okay. The meat wagon is coming."

As blood streamed from Paolo's body onto the sidewalk, Sal counted four bullet wounds in Paolo's chest. He ripped open Paolo's blood-soaked shirt. Sal's heart pounded inside his chest. He couldn't lose his best friend. Not like this.

Thea appeared near the front of the small crowd of onlookers. Tears streamed down her cheeks.

"Here, take this." She knelt down and handed Sal a clean towel and he pressed it against Paolo's wounds.

"Sal... you have to know..." Paolo wheezed between shallow breaths.

"It's okay, don't talk," Sal spoke low, his voice barely above a whisper. "You'll be fine."

Who would have done this to Paolo? Despite being linked to his cousin Marco, he was a good person. He didn't deserve this. When they were in school, Paolo and Sal were thick as thieves. They flirted with girls and played stickball. Then, when they got older, they snuck into the speakeasy and did a few jobs together. Sal could always count on his best friend.

Sal didn't want it to be real. He wiped his eyes which were brimming with tears.

As he lay in Sal's arms, Paolo struggled to catch his breath. His arms fell lifeless against his weak body.

"Sal... be careful..." Paolo panted.

"I'm fine," Sal said. "I wasn't hit. I'm fine." He folded and unfolded the now-bloody towel against Paolo's chest, trying in vain to stop the bleeding. The ambulance couldn't come soon enough.

"No... No... the dock guys..." Paolo gasped.

Sal stopped fumbling with the towel and gaped at his dying friend. "What dock guys? What are you talking about?" Sal shook his head realizing what he had just said. "Don't tell me the low down. Save your breath."

"I-- I-- have to tell you," Paolo whispered. Blood seeped from his nose.

"Don't talk." Sal could hear sirens in the distance. "The meat wagon is on its way. You'll be fine."

"Heroin... It's in..." Paolo coughed, spitting blood all over himself and Sal. "... the furniture."

"What? What do you mean it's in the furniture?" Sal shook his friend lightly. All the times he picked up furniture and delivered it, he simply assumed it was a furniture delivery. Every time he delivered it to the docks, Harry checked every piece thoroughly. Was this why Jack and Betsy Barden never helped Sal lift anything into his truck? Was Paolo's cousin Marco a major drug dealer in the city? Is that why the brute on the dock scampered away when Paolo showed up? Did Paolo get shot as payback for something Marco did?

How could Sal have been so naive? He didn't want to believe that he was in too deep with organized crime.

Paolo struggled to catch his breath, lying almost motionless in Sal's arms. Death was coming for him.

"You... did good... Sal," Paolo whispered. "Stay... good..." Paolo took his final breath in Sal's arms. His eyes glossed over and his breathing stopped.

"Don't go! Don't go!" Sal cried out. "You can't die!" To no avail, he shook Paolo's lifeless body, willing it to come back to life.

Next to Sal, Thea wailed as she wiped a stream of tears from her face with her apron.

Holding Paolo's body on his blood-soaked shirt, Sal sat there stunned. Stunned that Paolo was dead. Stunned that he watched his best friend die. Stunned he had no idea that he was a patsy for a drug ring.

Chapter 37

The South Side Sicilian neighborhood came in droves for Paolo's funeral at Santa Maria. Black-clad mourners filled the pews to pay their respects, clutching Mass cards and rosary beads. An abundance of floral garlands and wreaths cascaded around the altar, permeating the church with sweet aromas. Candles twinkled, casting an angelic ambiance onto the scene. The organist played a haunting melody. Paolo's wooden casket lay open so that the bereaved could kiss his cheek or forehead in a final goodbye. In the vestibule, Father Lazzeri greeted everyone, directing them to Paolo's parents in the front pew.

Dressed in his best black suit, Sal escorted his parents into the church. Bartolomeo and Theresa shuffled down the aisle as Sal absorbed everything. He had been to many funerals; the idea of death didn't shock him. But this was the first time he came to a friend's. His best friend. Except for almost breaking down as he held his dying friend, Sal had not cried. He was in disbelief that Paolo was gone. He was numb and empty. Paolo's murder made the front page of the paper the previous day. No one was arrested, and no one knew anything. Typical for organized crime. The police had talked to Sal but they had no leads. Paolo's nefarious killer could go free, disappearing into the depths of the city forever.

Sal couldn't fathom not talking to Paolo ever again. Who would he get breakfast with at the diner? Who would laugh at his dumb jokes? Who would he bum cigarettes from? Who would he talk to about sweet dames? He slowly approached the casket, afraid to touch Paolo's lifeless body. Sal stared at the life that was cut short, a shadow of its once vibrant self. A pack of cigarettes and Paolo's favorite lighter were placed in the casket to calm his soul.

He leaned over the edge of the casket and whispered, "Goodbye, *goombah*."

Sal found Paolo's mother and father in the front pew. Paolo's mother wore a long black dress and a black veil that covered her face. His father wore a black double-breasted suit with a matching tie. Their puffy eyes were red with tears as they mourned their youngest son. Sal embraced them and held tight.

"You were with our Paolo when he died," Paolo's father spoke, pulling away from Sal.

Sal nodded.

"Did he suffer?"

"No, *signore*." Sal remembered Paolo gasping for his last breaths, but he didn't want to tarnish the virtuous memory that Paolo's parents held. "I will miss him."

"He with God now," Paolo's mother murmured. Under her black veil, she dabbed her face with a white handkerchief. Sal couldn't help but notice the stark contrast of colors.

Sal genuflected and headed to a few pews behind them, settling in next to his parents. He grasped his mother's gloved hand.

Father Lazzeri stood at the altar, raised his arms above his head, and quieted the grieving congregation.

"Our son Paolo has been called home." He spoke for the next twenty minutes, leading the faithful in prayer and liturgy. He performed the rest of the Mass, singing Paolo's praises.

After the Mass was over, six pallbearers dressed in matching black suits hoisted Paolo's closed casket on their shoulders and carried it out of the church to the waiting hearse. The mourners filed out of Santa Maria into a procession as the chapel bell echoed into the surrounding city blocks. They followed the hearse by foot to Paolo's gravesite a few streets away.

At the cemetery, Sal joined the other grievers, walked up to the casket, and tossed a handful of dirt on it. Still numb, Sal couldn't shed a tear. Paolo's mother placed a single rose on her son's final resting place. After the closing remarks and prayers, most of the attending mourners headed to Paolo's parents' house.

A few minutes later, Sal entered their home and encountered wall-to-wall people talking, praying, hugging, crying, and eating. When they learned the news of Paolo's passing, neighbors and relatives had brought casserole dishes filled with pasta, chicken, eggplant, tomatoes, and desserts. Bottles of homemade wine filled an entire table in the front room.

Many of Paolo's relatives stopped Sal as he wandered through the home, offering their condolences and wondering how Sal handled Paolo dying in his arms.

"Did he speak to you?" they asked. "Did you try to save him? Do you know who shot him?"

Exhausted, Sal gave the same answers over and over again. Yes, Paolo spoke to him. Yes, he tried to save Paolo. No, he didn't know who shot Paolo. It had been a long day and Sal was drained.

Though he had no appetite, Sal knew he needed to refuel. He headed for a table full of fruit and homemade bread and grabbed a plate.

A young man, not older than fifteen, had the same idea and joined Sal at the table picking up strawberries, melon, grapes, olives, and a slice of bread.

"My Ma told me you were there when he died," the teenager said to Sal. He was as tall as Sal but barely filled out his suit. He reminded Sal of his oldest nephew.

"Yeah." Sal silently willed the boy not to ask the same questions he had been answering all afternoon. He was tired, empty, and raw. Drowning in his grief, he hadn't slept in three days.

"Did his chest explode? Was there a lot of blood? Did you see his organs?" The young man's eyes filled with morbid curiosity.

Sal had to stop himself from chuckling at the teenager's unfiltered questions. He welcomed the change from the hushed and sombered conversations he had been having with others in the house.

"No. Paolo's chest didn't explode," Sal explained. "But I did see a lot of blood."

"Was it everywhere?" The young man popped a strawberry into his mouth.

Sal shrugged. He wasn't sure how much this kid wanted to know. Why was he so fascinated? Sal, however, never wanted to see that much blood ever again. Paolo's murder would haunt his nightmares for months.

"I'm gonna be a doctor someday," the boy volunteered. "I hope to get into Johns Hopkins. That's if my Ma and Pop will let me go to Maryland."

"Do you have good grades?" Sal asked, welcoming the change in topic.

"Yeah. Tops of my class at Tilden Tech."

"That's where I went." Sal smiled, the first time all day, at the boy's fraternal connection.

"Yeah, I know," the young man said. "You went with my cousin Paolo."

"What's your name?" Sal inquired. "Maybe I can put in a good word for you."

"Marco."

Sal blinked. This scrawny kid was Paolo's cousin Marco? The same cousin who Paolo constantly talked about. The cousin who got them into the speakeasy for the first time and set Sal up with several jobs. The cousin who paid Sal in cash. The cousin who ran an underground heroin smuggling operation. The cousin who most likely got Paolo killed. There had to be a mistake.

"Are you his *only* cousin named Marco?" Sal arched an eyebrow, hoping for a logical explanation. He had several cousins with the same name, so maybe Paolo did too.

"As far as I know," Marco replied. He popped another strawberry in his mouth, reminding Sal of Paolo's blood.

Sal's brain stuttered for an instant and he dropped his plate of fruit onto the floor. He stood there, stunned, as Marco scrambled to the floor to pick up the scattered debris.

"Are you okay, Sal?" Marco stood back up and handed Sal a plate of dirt-covered food. "You don't look so good."

"I-- I--" Sal stammered, the plate of food tottering in his hand. His eyes couldn't focus as every part of his body paused waiting for his words to catch up. His chest rose and fell with rapid breaths. He needed to sit down.

"I'm gonna go get someone," Marco offered and took off into the crowd of guests.

In a fog, Sal somehow placed his plate of food on the table and fell backward against it. He wanted to vomit as if he was three sheets to the wind, but he felt stone-cold sober. He clutched his stomach as things started to make sense. Stumbling, Sal found his way to the back door and pushed his way through, hearing Marco tell someone in the distance to come help.

The back alley was empty except for a stray dog sniffing for scraps. Sal gulped in pockets of fresh air as he clung to the iron handrail.

"It was you, Paolo! It was always you!" Sal shook a tight fist to the heavens. "How could you not tell me? How could you do this to me?"

With pinched tight lips, Sal stared up to the billowy clouds as if he was waiting for an answer.

"You were the one who connected me with Joe Aiello! You're the one who that ruffian at the docks was afraid of! You were the one who wanted to keep a low profile!" Sal shouted upwards. "It was never your cousin! It was always you! You got yourself killed!" He let out a forceful breath.

Sal rubbed his throbbing temple and his jaw tightened. Anger seared through him. How could he be such a fool? How did he not know all this about his best friend? How could Paolo use him like that? He loved and hated Paolo.

In an instant, Sal ran off down the alley, his dress shoes clacking against the cement. He was searching for something, anything, to make sense of it all.

Chapter 38

September 1932

With a sweaty forehead, Sal awoke from his nightmare with a start. He had dreamt that someone was chasing him down a dark alley, shooting at him. The hired goon cornered him, raised a Tommy Gun, pulled the trigger and--

In a panic, Sal patted his chest, checking for bullet holes. Fear clawed at him.

"You okay, Sal." Bartolomeo soothed him as he sat next to Sal on the couch in their front room. "What you dream about?"

"Someone..." Sal spoke above a whisper. "Someone was going to shoot me." Even though Paolo had been dead for two months, Sal continued to have nightmares. The Chicago police investigated the drive-by shooting, asking Sal several times for his eyewitness testimony, but no one was arrested.

"No one shoot you," Bartolomeo spoke. "You here. You home. You safe." He placed a light blanket over Sal.

"Thanks, Pop."

Sal glanced around the room. Everything was in its place. His hat was on the coat rack. His Ma and Pop's shoes were placed neatly near the door. Opened curtains let in a blaze of end-of-summer sunshine.

Father and son sat in silence for a moment.

For the past two months, Sal had hardly left the house. He lost his desire to enjoy everything the bustling city had to offer. Rose, Charlie, and Annie had brought over their families a few times to visit. Sal appreciated seeing his innocent nieces and nephews, but, as soon as they left, he curled back up on the couch. Even when Phil jotted over to share his newspaper, Sal could have cared less.

Sal appreciated his siblings' concern for him, but his heart ached. His best friend had lied to him for years and now he was dead. Sal couldn't even confront Paolo to get the whole truth. Sal might never know who killed Paolo. It was likely some goon seeking revenge for a drug deal gone wrong.

"What you want to eat?" Bartolomeo broke the silence. "I make for you."

"I'm not hungry, Pop." Sal slowly sat up on the couch and rubbed his bloodshot eyes.

"No. You eat." Bartolomeo pointed a crooked finger at his son. In his early sixties now, Bartolomeo still loved to cook for his family. "Food help you."

"Just some antipasto is fine." Sal shrugged. He wasn't sure if he would eat but wanted to placate his Pop.

Bartolomeo stepped toward the kitchen. He stopped and turned back to Sal. "Paolo good boy."

"Thanks, Pop." Like many people, Bartolomeo didn't know the truth about Paolo's corrupt lifestyle. Sal thought it best to keep him, and the rest of his family, blissfully ignorant.

Exhausted, Sal laid back down, pulling the blanket over himself.

Fifteen minutes later, Bartolomeo called that the food was ready.

Sal joined his Pop in the kitchen. His Ma was at the church sewing clothes for the poor with other wives. Despite his parents' protests, Sal couldn't bring himself to go to Mass with them. He knew if he stepped inside Santa Maria, the place where he said goodbye to Paolo, he'd cry for days. He still hadn't cried because he failed to grieve completely.

Bartolomeo placed a large bowl of olives, anchovies, pepperoncini, artichoke hearts, cheeses, and pickled meats in the center of the table. Even though it was only the two of them eating, the food was enough to feed six or seven. He spooned some onto a plate for Sal and himself.

Sal grabbed a loaf of his mother's homemade bread from the Hoosier cabinet. Theresa had made it before she went to Santa Maria, and the room still lingered with the sweet smell of baked bread. Sal poured two glasses of wine from his father's batch and brought them to the table.

Finding his appetite, Sal enjoyed his father's antipasto. "This is good, Pop."

"You make it with me next time," Bartolomeo directed. "I teach you."

Sal smiled weakly. "You've already taught me a lot."

"I teach you not to be gangster," Bartolomeo spoke. He put a forkful of olives into his mouth, then continued. "You live simple life. You cook. You work real job. You find wife and you have *bambinos*. You take care of *famiglia*. You not be like men who kill Paolo."

"You're right, Pop." Sal smiled again, with admiration for his dad. Sal needed to give up the broads at the speakeasy for good. He would never find a good wife there. With Paolo dead, Sal swore he'd never work an illegal job again. He didn't want to die.

At 23, it was time for Sal to settle down.

Chapter 39

January 29, 1933

Snow blasted the city of Chicago. Brave residents stumbled off sidewalks as the winter wind roared at them from all sides. Many men had shaved their mustaches because they had formed blocks of ice on their faces. Cars and trolleys halted in the snowbanks, causing massive traffic jams and annoyed travelers. The city attempted to pile the mounds of snow in the river, but it instantly froze. Boats were stranded in the ice. Ropes, strung across State Street, near Marshall Field's, helped pedestrians walk erect through whipping winds.

At home, sitting next to the oil-based radiator, Sal listened to the Black Hawks game play on the radio. Paul Thompson and Tom Cook were their leading scorers, but neither player could put the puck in the net against the New York Americans.

"Hold off those New York bums!" Sal yelled to goalie Chuck Gardiner, even though his cheering fell on deaf ears. The Black Hawks were losing three to nothing.

"Salvatore!" Bartolomeo appeared from the hallway and put a finger to his lips against his bushy mustache. "Quiet. Your Mama is sleeping."

"Sorry, Pop." Sal twisted the radio volume lower.

"You come with us to church tomorrow." Bartolomeo poked a finger at his youngest son.

"But Pop, we went to Mass this morning." A month earlier, during Advent, Sal finally found the strength to go to church again. Six months had passed since Paolo had been killed.

"No Mass," Bartolomeo explained. "We meet nice girl for you. Her family new here. They come from Sicily." Bartolomeo waved his arms around, gesturing to their outside neighborhood that was now covered in snow.

Sal pondered the idea. He hadn't been out with a dame since before Paolo died. And even then, the broad wasn't good enough to bring around his parents. The last nice girl he dated was Sophia. That was four years earlier on Valentine's Day and he hadn't seen her since she had slapped him when they encountered Mae on the sidewalk. He hadn't had any contact with her since.

"Okay, Pop. What time are we going?"

"You go when I say."

Sal chuckled at his father's dry humor.

Once Upon a Time in Chicago

* * * *

The next evening, Sal, Bartolomeo, and Theresa trudged through the slush to Santa Maria to meet his possible suitress. The wind had died down, leaving glistening snow banks on the edge of the sidewalks. Under his overcoat, Sal wore a white V-neck sweater, a shirt and tie, and high-waisted tweed slacks. He wanted to look snazzy but not overdress with a suit. Excited and nervous, he hoped the woman in question spoke English. What would they talk about? How could he manage to talk to any woman with his parents around?

The Scavuzzo family entered the church and headed downstairs to the social hall where men of the congregation often played cribbage. When they stepped into the large room, they spotted Father Lazzeri at a table speaking to a man, a woman, and their daughter who appeared to be in her early 20s. The young woman was blessed with a headful of almost-black hair and olive skin. Her heart-shaped face and dainty nose accented her alluring brown eyes. She wore a light-blue dress and a matching cloche hat. Sal smiled to himself, pleased that she was so attractive.

Father Lazzeri stopped talking to the family and stood up.

"Ah, *Signore* and *Signora* Scavuzzo." The priest embraced them, kissing them on both cheeks. He nodded toward Sal. "Salvatore."

He motioned to the waiting family. "This is Giovanni and Valentina Cammareri and their daughter Angelina."

Angelina, Sal thought. A lovely name for a lovely girl.

"*Signore* and *Signora* Cammareri, this is Bartolomeo and Theresa Scavuzzo and their son Salvatore," Father Lazzeri spoke again.

Following his parents' lead, Sal sat at the table next to the priest. Angelina sat across from him, placing her hands on her lap. Sal found it cute when she averted her gaze from him.

"The Cammareris came through Ellis Island a few weeks ago and have decided to settle here in Chicago," Father Lazzeri explained to Sal and his parents. "Since you have been here for twenty-five years, I had hoped that you could show them around our neighborhood and get them acquainted."

"We proud to do so," Bartolomeo spoke for his family. He sat taller in his chair, maximizing his short stature. "What village in Sicily you from?"

"Misterbianco in Catania," Giovanni answered. "We sell *vigneto* to move here. We want learn English. Talk like *Ahmedigans*."

Bartolomeo smiled broadly and raised his hands in praise toward Sal. "My son Salvatore help. He teach your Angelina and she teach you. He went to college."

Sal took heed to his father's volunteering and sat up straighter. "Yes, of course, I would love to help. We can start right away." He smiled at Angelina and she sheepishly smiled back.

Theresa and Valentina exchanged a conspiratorial glance about the matchmaking of their children.

Chapter 40

The next evening, Sal made his way to the Cammareri homestead with a few newspapers tucked under the arm of his overcoat. He was anxious to spend some time with Angelina. He couldn't come on too strong, especially because she didn't speak much English.

The Cammareris lived on the first floor of a two-story flat on West 25th Street, two blocks from Shields Avenue. A bay window greeted the street through red brick that encompassed the entire building. A semi-enclosed porch protected guests from the unpredictable wind.

Sal hopped up the steps and rapped on the front door.

"*Buona sera, Signore* Cammareri," Sal said to Angelina's father when he opened the door.

"*Benvenuto*." Giovanni caught himself and shook his head. "I say…"

"'Welcome'. You say 'welcome,'" Sal assisted his new friend.

"*Grazie*. Er, thank you." Giovanni smiled and led Sal inside to the foyer. "That I learn."

"Don't worry, Signore Cammareri," Sal reassured him, "you'll be a pro in no time."

"Pro?"

Sal grimaced when he realized he said a word that might not be understood and embarrass Signore Cammareri. He wanted to show extreme respect to the man. Diligence and patience were expected.

"I mean you'll be perfect. *Perfetto*."

Valentina entered the foyer and pointed to Sal's coat. "I take."

Sal shrugged out of his overcoat but kept the newspapers. "Thank you *Signora* Cammareri. *Grazie*."

"You're… wel… come…" She smiled, pleased that she knew the correct English term.

Giovanni and Valentina led Sal to their kitchen, where Angelina sat at the table studying a book. She glanced up when they came into the room.

"Welcome to our home," she said to Sal.

Before Sal could answer, Angelina waved a hand at her parents. "It's good, Mama and Papa. *Bene*." They turned and left the young adults in the kitchen.

She spoke to Sal, "Please. Sit."

Sal took a seat at the table across from Angelina and set the newspapers next to him. With her hair flowing down her back, she appeared more casual this time.

"You speak exceptional English," Sal said. "Maybe you don't need my help?"

"I studied the King's English while I was in London last year."

"What were you doing there?"

"Taking classes at King's College. My parents sent me with the profits they earned from their vineyard. You aren't the only one who went to college."

Angelina smirked at Sal. He liked her already.

"If you already know English, why am I here? Can't you teach your parents how to speak?" Sal wondered out loud. He glanced at the newspapers, realizing he wouldn't need them as reference material to teach Angelina.

"I am," Angelina admitted. "I think they wanted me to meet a nice boy here. They worry I read too much."

"I guess Father Lazzeri chose me?" Sal raised an eyebrow.

"I overheard you were the only single man left."

Sal never considered that. He had never paid attention to any of the other young men at Santa Maria's. While he and Paolo were out on the town, he guessed that their classmates had found nice dames, got married, and started families of their own. He was the only one left.

"Would you like to go out with me sometime? Maybe to the theater?" Sal pointed to the newspaper next to him. "There's a new Cary Grant movie out."

"Yes. That would be nice." Angelina nodded.

Sal and Angelina chatted for the next hour, only being interrupted by her mother and father to make sure their conversation remained virtuous.

He left there and headed home, content that he was on the right path.

* * * *

A few days later, Sal returned to the Cammareri household and asked for Angelina to go on their date. As they walked toward the trolley stop, Sal assisted Angelina around slush puddles so that she wouldn't ruin her shoes. He held her arm in the crook of his elbow as she talked about the works of Socrates and the decline of the American economy. Sal didn't always grasp what Angelina pondered, but he liked her company.

As they boarded the trolley, Sal dropped two dimes into the coin slot and guided Angelina to an open seat for two.

"Do you believe that we are real and we are part of a real world?" Angelina philosophized, pointing a finger to her chin.

"Yeah, I guess so," Sal answered. He held her close next to him.

"Do you believe that there is a force or greater reality that is responsible for the existence of the universe?"

"Didn't God create the universe in seven days?" Sal recalled from his time spent at Santa Maria.

"Charles Darwin argued that with his theory of evolution," Angelina countered.

She continued talking about metaphysics and social philosophy as Sal nodded in agreement until they reached their stop.

"This is where we get off," Sal interrupted Angelina. He stood in the aisle, reached for her hand, and led her to the sidewalk. They approached the New Palace Theater. The golden marquee read: Cary Grant and Mae West in *She Done Him Wrong*. Sal bought their tickets and escorted Angelina to their seats.

"I hope you like the movie," Sal whispered as the lights went down.

"I will. I'm with you." Angelina grasped Sal's hand in hers.

Chapter 41

For the next few months, Sal and Angelina spent a lot of time together. They shared ice cream at the local soda fountain. They danced the lindy at the public dance hall because Sal felt that Angelina was too classy for the speakeasy. On a rare warm March afternoon, they admired the animals at the Lincoln Park Zoo. They studied astronomy at Adler Planetarium, the first planetarium built in the Western Hemisphere three years earlier. At Shedd Aquarium, they sat in front of a big fish tank pondering underwater life.

Every time they went somewhere, Sal learned something new about his city even though he had lived in Chicago all of his life. He appreciated Angelina's desire to expand her mind and articulate what she had learned. Sal found her to be confident, cultured, and curious. She was different from any other woman he had ever met. They shared the occasional kiss and held hands.

Sal wasn't sure if he loved Angelina, but he was certain that he liked her. She helped him move on from Paolo's death, thinking about living a good life that his Pop wanted him to have. Sal wanted love.

In mid-April of 1933, Bartolomeo invited the Cammareris over for Easter dinner.

"All my children and grandchildren come," Bartolomeo explained to Giovanni at the weekly men's card game at Santa Maria. "You meet them. I cook!"

"Enough room in your home?" Giovanni's English had improved over the past few months thanks to his daughter and Sal.

"*Si,*" Bartolomeo answered. "Always room. Theresa finds guests."

Both families spent Easter morning at Mass. Afterward, Giovanni, Valentina, and Angelina arrived at the Scavuzzo household. Sal and Bartolomeo greeted them at the door, taking their hats and coats.

"Meet my *famiglia.*" Bartolomeo gestured toward the many people chatting on the couch. Children scuttled across the floor, and similar sounds floated from the kitchen.

Bartolomeo pointed as his family members wandered in and out of the room. "There's Charles and his wife Frances. Their kids Theresa, Joseph, Charles Junior, Betty, and Bobby. Then Rosa and her husband Michael. Their kids Ignazio, Santa, Carmen, Barth, Raymond, and Michael Junior. Then Antoinette--Annie-- and her husband Stephen. Their daughters Annette, Theresa, and Delores. Phillipe and his wife Joyce. Their daughter Theresa Rose. Then Salvatore. And my *bambino* Faye and her husband Nicholas.”

Angelina's eyes widened at the many names and Sal hustled over to her. “Don't worry, you don't have to remember everyone.”

“Good,” she whispered.

Giovanni spoke, “We have many *famiglia* in Misterbianco. Here like there.” He laughed with delight.

Bartolomeo led his guests to the dining area where a table lined with sixteen chairs filled the space. Theresa wiped her hands on an apron over her clothes, hurried over to her guests, and embraced them. “*Benvenuto. Benvenuto.*” She motioned for them to sit. A steaming platter of lamb with potatoes, peas, fava beans, artichokes, green beans, spinach, and asparagus took center stage on the table. Multiple bowls of pasta and fresh Easter bread surrounded the display.

“Why does your mama not speak much English when all of you do?” Angelina asked Sal as they followed their parents to the table.

“She never felt the need to learn, I guess,” Sal explained. “She understands us for the most part and we translate for her. Maybe she figured she was too old to learn.”

“My papa is 50 and he is learning English,” Angelina said. “No one is ever too old to learn something.”

Sal's siblings and their spouses gathered at the large table. In the kitchen, his nieces and nephews argued about where to sit.

Bartolomeo led the group in the blessing.

"Did you lose a bet?" Phil asked Angelina as he served himself some pasta that had found its way in front of him.

"I beg your pardon." She arched an eyebrow at him.

Sal stifled a laugh as he knew where his brother's question was headed.

"You know, did you lose at something and have to pay up by going out with my brother?" Phil clarified. "Because that's the only way he could have found a nice dame like you."

"Phil, be nice," Joyce admonished her husband.

"No." Angelina nodded toward Sal. "Sal has been a perfect gentleman."

"My brother?" Charlie pointed at Sal with a fork. "He's a twit. You gotta watch yourself with him."

Angelina cocked her head at Charlie and narrowed her eyes.

"He's joking," Sal said to Angelina.

"Look at 'im," Phil rejoined the roast, much to the chagrin of his wife. "He's a Duke of Limbs. I bet any clown at the circus could lift more than him."

The brothers roared in laughter.

"Behave!" Bartolomeo interrupted the ruckus, raising his hand toward his oldest sons. "We have guests."

"Sorry, Pop," Charlie and Phil said in unison, trying to hide their smirks.

"Angelina," Annie spoke, "you'll have to excuse my brothers. They can be lug-heads but they mean well."

After dinner, the families enjoyed Theresa's cassata cake. The scrumptious dessert featured a yellow cake with sweetened ricotta cream, candied fruit, chocolate, and nuts. Bartolomeo poured his homemade wine into glasses.

"This is delicious, *Signora* Scavuzzo," Angelina told Sal's mother. Realizing Sal's mother didn't understand what she had said, Angelina spoke again, "*è delizioso.*"

"*Grazie. Grazie.*" Theresa smiled wide at her young guest.

At the end of the evening, Sal escorted the Cammareris to the front door.

While Giovanni assisted Valentina into her coat, Sal helped Angelina with hers.

"Why are your brothers so mean to you?" Angelina asked as she buttoned up.

"Ah, them," Sal chuckled, "they're having a little fun. Like Annie said earlier, they mean well. You just don't understand because you're an only child. You'll get used to it."

"If you say so," Angelina replied.

Sal squeezed her hands. "I'll see you in a few days. I'm happy that you want to go to the White Sox game with me."

"It will be my first baseball game," Angelina replied. "So, you'll have to explain the rules to me."

Sal laughed. Settling down with a family now appealed to him. "I'd love to."

Chapter 42

May 27, 1933

"Let's go to the World's Fair, Sal!" Angelina gushed as they walked hand in hand down Shields Avenue. "It opens today. I read in the paper that it is being called 'A Century of Progress' and an exposition of the greatest era of the world's scientific and industrial history."

"Sure, sweetheart. Whatever you want."

Chicago had been preparing for the fair for the past four years. The fair planned to stay open until November. This was a job that called for men and women of vision and civic spirit. Even during the national financial crisis, the fair was developed without any taxation imposed upon already heavily burdened residents. The city expected to lure one hundred thousand attendees to help the economy by charging five dollars per person. The exposition encompassed two dozen city blocks along Lake Michigan.

"I want to see the pageant of transportation and the transformation of electricity." Angelina broke free of Sal's grasp and skipped down the street. "The drama of agriculture and the fairyland of flowers."

"And we can ride the Towering Sky-Ride I've read about," Sal called after her as he hurried to keep up. The first-ever sky-ride cable connected two steel towers 1850 feet apart and rose 628 feet into the sky. Rocket cars offered a thrilling ride across Lake Michigan's lagoons. "And the Goodyear blimp. And I heard Dixie Blandy wants to set a world record for sitting on top of a flagpole there."

Sal had learned over the past few months that he and Angelina liked different things, but they found a mutual respect for one another and he enjoyed her company. Angelina discovered his fondness for the poetic works of Carl Sandburg and Robert Frost. In turn, Sal taught her the finer points of the elusive grand slam. He would go with Angelina to the World's Fair and she would accompany him to the baseball league's first All-Star game at Comiskey Park.

The next evening, Sal and Angelina entered the fair curious and eager. The bombardment of color and light created the illusion of stepping within a giant jewel. Its myriad facets flashed countless rays of beauty. Millions of lights flashed skyward a symphony of illumination reflecting off Lake Michigan as if progress was speaking to them.

Chrysler and General Motors displayed the latest models of their cars. The Parade of States featured a striking procession that told the story of the great country's history. Dramatic and exotic displays came from foreign nations - Italy, Mexico, Denmark, Luxemburg, China, Morocco. Westinghouse implored visitors to see the Hall of Miracles promoting the latest developments in electrical science. The Home Planning Hall highlighted the new air-cooled Electrolux gas refrigerator. On the Midway, the Old Plantation Show brought delight with Siamese twins and the Dionne quintuplets. Log rollers battled each other on the banks of Lake Michigan.

"There's no way we'll see it all tonight," Sal said.

"Then we'll come back again and again," Angelina chattered. Even in the throng of people surrounding them, she managed to swirl around in excitement. Attendees wandered in every direction fascinated with the concepts around them.

Sal grasped Angelina's hand and let the fair envelop them.

Chapter 43

July 28, 1933

"What a buncha bums," Sal muttered to himself as he perused the sports section of the *Chicago Tribune*. He sat at his kitchen table nursing a cup of coffee. "Eight games in a row."

"What you say, Salvatore?" Bartolomeo entered the room to prepare lunch. The perpetual scent of garlic accompanied him.

"Nothin', Pop," Sal sighed. "The White Sox lost again."

"Have hope."

Sal offered a weak smile.

"Like hope for you and Angelina," Bartolomeo said. "She nice girl."

"Yeah, Pop, she is."

"You can marry her. I approve. She Sicilian." Bartolomeo pointed to his chest with pride.

Even though Sal wasn't sure if he wanted to marry Angelina, he knew what his father meant. It helped that Angelina was Sicilian. Bartolomeo was suspicious of anyone who didn't come from their island. All of his brothers and sisters married Sicilians. If Sal ever considered marrying a dame who wasn't Sicilian, he might be banned from the house.

Angelina was a good option to marry. She was smart, nice, confident, classy, and was patient around Sal's nieces and nephews. Were all those good qualities enough to want to marry her? Because of Angelina, Sal had no desire to go to the speakeasy or flirt with other dames. He liked her, but he still wasn't sure if he loved her. She didn't make his heart race and he didn't stop to think about her when she wasn't with him. She would make someone a great wife. Sal wasn't sure if she would make a great wife for *him*.

"Thanks, Pop," Sal said. "I appreciate that."

"You see Angelina tonight?"

"Yeah, we're going back to the Fair," Sal answered. "We've been there three times already and still haven't seen it all. But Dixie Blandy is still sitting on top of that flagpole."

"*Idiota,*" Bartolomeo muttered and gathered his pots to cook.

* * * *

When Sal picked up Angelina at her house later that night, she held a small leather book in her hand.

"Before we go to the fair tonight, can we make a stop?" she asked.

"Sure. What do you want to do?"

"I borrowed this book of Shakespearean sonnets from a woman I know from Santa Maria and I'd like to return it."

"Where does she live?" Sal asked.

"A couple of blocks west on Stewart Avenue."

After Angelina said goodbye to her parents, Sal led her to Stewart Avenue. Once on the street, Angelina guided Sal to the correct house, talking the whole way.

"Shakespeare uses Iambic Pentameter in his sonnets. There are fourteen lines in a Shakespearean sonnet. The first twelve lines are divided into three quatrains with four lines each," Angelina rattled off.

Sal listened intently, not paying much attention to where they were headed.

Moments later, they reached the front door of the house in question. Angelina knocked on the front door.

An older woman, similar in age to their mothers, answered the door. She wore a dark dress that reached the floor and her greying hair was pulled up with pins on her head.

"*Buona sera, Signora* Catalano,*"* Angelina spoke to the woman and held out the book. "I'm here to return this."

"*Buona sera,* Angelina. Thank you." The woman received the book and nodded to Sal. "Who is this with you?"

"This is Sal," Angelina spoke. "I told you about him."

"Ah yes," Signora Catalano replied. "Please come in. My nieces are here and I want you to join us." She held the door open as Angelina and Sal entered her home.

Once inside, Signora Catalano directed Sal and Angelina to sit down on the sofa. A steaming carafe perched atop a warming plate on the coffee table in front of them. On the mantle above the now-silent fireplace, Sal spotted a row of books with titles from Pearl S. Buck, Aldous Huxley, William Faulkner, and Gertrude Stein. He could hear a conversation in the adjoining kitchen.

Signora Catalano focused her attention on a young woman facing away from them, who was lowering the volume on an oak Silverton floor radio. She tapped the auburn-haired young lady on the shoulder to turn around.

"Angelina and Sal," Signora Catalano spoke, "I'd like you to meet my niece--"

"Sophia!" Sal gasped.

"You two know each other?" Angelina pointed a finger between Sal and Sophia, grasping the connection.

"Yes." Sophia sat in the nearby art-deco padded chair and crossed her legs. "Sal and I used to go steady." She casually flipped a ringed left hand into the air. "But that was years ago. Before I met my husband."

"Four years ago, if I remember correctly," Sal added. He was thankful that Sophia didn't supply any details on how she ended their relationship to Angelina. She might have left him right then and there - like Sophia did on that cold sidewalk. He liked to think that Angelina made him a changed man. "How long have you been married?"

"A year next month," Sophia replied.

"Congratulations." Angelina offered her hand to Sophia.

Two more young women entered the living room holding teacups. The stockier one had dark hair like Angelina and the thin one was blonde. Sal caught himself staring a second too long at the attractive blonde. They sat in empty chairs on the other side of the coffee table.

Signora Catalano spoke again, "I'd like you to meet my other niece Jenny." She pointed to the homely brunette. "And her friend Florence." She pointed to the blonde. "They came here on the train by themselves all the way from Pittsburgh, Pennsylvania, to see the World's Fair."

Florence, Sal repeated her name to himself. She was a beautiful and lovely woman. Sal's heart nearly stopped. Every part of him craved her. Even with Angelina sitting next to him, he couldn't stop staring at Florence. He inched closer to her.

"How do you like the Fair so far? How long are you in town?" Angelina asked all at once.

"It's been wonderful. So lovely," Jenny replied. "We leave in two days to go back home."

"Do you live in the downtown part of Pittsburgh like we do here?" Sal asked. He wanted to learn everything about Florence.

"No," she answered. "We are from a small city called Jeannette 30 miles east of the city. We took the train from there to Pittsburgh and then from there to here."

Sal's infatuation grew with every word that Florence spoke. Her voice sounded like doves singing in high trees. He leaned forward to listen more intently to what she would say next.

"Jenny and Florence went to college together at the University of Pittsburgh," Sophia pointed out.

"What did you study? Greek? Latin?" Angelina wanted to know.

"I studied Education," Florence answered. "I've been a schoolteacher in a coal-patch town called Crabtree for four years now." When she tucked a loose strand of blonde hair behind her ear, Sal followed her lovely hands with his eyes from start to finish.

He quickly did the math in his head. If Florence had been teaching for four years, that meant she graduated from college in 1929, which made her 26 years old. Two years *older* than him. He unconsciously parted his lips.

"The students in the two-room schoolhouse are pretty poor, so we bring them lunch and clothing when we can," Jenny added.

"My parents own a store that supplies everything," Florence said.

She folded one leg over the other, exposing her curvy legs.

Sal hoped Florence did that on purpose. He briefly thought back to the dolls at the speakeasy, knowing they made moves like that to attract men. He couldn't take his eyes off of Florence's gams.

"I have a few things you can take back with you," Signora Catalano replied.

"Thank you," Florence said.

Signora Catalano focused her attention on Angelina. "Do you have plans tomorrow night?"

"I don't think so," Angelina replied.

"Robert Frost will be reading his poetry at Le Petit Gourmet on North Michigan Boulevard. Would you like to come?"

"Sal and I would love to come!" Angelina gushed.

"What about you?" Sal gestured to Florence and Jenny. "Will you be going too?" Even with Angelina nearby, he wanted to spend as much time as possible with Florence before she went back home to Jeannette. Her sparkling green eyes captivated him and caused him to forget why he was out with Angelina that night to begin with.

"No," Jenny replied, "we want to spend our last day here at the Fair. There are still so many things we haven't seen."

"Oh, right, the Fair," Sal remembered out loud.

"Speaking of that…" Angelina stood from the couch. "Sal and I are going there tonight." She offered a hand toward Sophia, Jenny, and Florence. "It was lovely to meet you."

Begrudgingly, Sal stood up and joined Angelina.

"Yes." He held Florence's soft hand a second longer and smiled a silly grin. He could have sworn her cheeks blushed. "It was lovely to meet you."

Chapter 44

A few days later, Sal still couldn't get Florence out of his head. If Angelina hadn't pushed them to leave Signora Catalano's house, Sal would have stayed all night to talk with Florence. He wanted to know more about her. Did she have any brothers or sisters? What did her father do? Had she traveled anywhere else besides Chicago? What was her last name? Sal surprised himself that he was so infatuated with a woman and didn't even know her last name.

That morning, his mind had wandered to Florence so much that he forgot to put a sock on. He stomped into the kitchen and his Pop asked him why he wore two shoes but only one sock. He now sat at the kitchen table, reading the morning paper, but couldn't concentrate on the words in front of him. Sal barely knew Florence. She made him want to settle down. Suddenly, he wanted to have children. With her. He'd go the straight and narrow. Sal would change everything for Florence.

Sal wished Paolo was still alive. Paolo would have said Sal was "dizzy with a dame." He couldn't talk to his Pop about Florence. Bartolomeo had already said he approved of Angelina. But Sal couldn't marry Angelina. Especially not now. There was only one person who Sal could talk to about Florence.

"I'll be back in a little while, Pop," Sal called to Bartolomeo who was in a back room. Sal didn't wait for a response, grabbed his billfold, and headed out the door.

After dropping a dime into the coin slot on the trolley, Sal was headed uptown to see a familiar face. Sal disembarked at Jackson Boulevard, skipping toward Lou Mitchell's along with the sweet refrains of the street peddlers.

A group of boys huddled on the sidewalk shooting marbles. Sal stopped and leaned over the shoulder of the boy closest to him. "Go for the big green one."

"Thanks, Mister," the boy called as Sal stood upright and continued on his path.

Sal pushed open the shiny doors to Lou Mitchell's and the bells jingled. He shimmied in their melody and headed toward the counter.

"'Morning, Thea."

"Aren't you a sight for sore eyes!" She leaned over the counter as far as she could go and wrapped her arms around Sal. "I haven't seen you since Paolo's funeral a year ago."

"It's been a long time." Sal took a seat in front of her. A few other patrons filled the diner. "I'm sorry I haven't been around."

"It's okay, sweetie. I understand." Thea grabbed an empty coffee cup from the clean rack and placed it in front of Sal. "What can I get for you today?"

"How about some of your famous pot roast?"

Thea called back to the grill for an order of pot roast and then turned back and studied Sal. "You look different. What happened?"

"What do you mean I look different?" Sal patted himself down. "My clothes are the same. I haven't grown a beard or anything."

"I don't know." Thea put a finger to her chin. "Like you're the cat who swallowed the canary."

Sal grinned and leaned forward on the counter as if he was telling Thea a secret. "I met a dame. A real classy one. A looker."

"Not one of those floozies you and Paolo used to meet at the speakeasy I hope?"

"How did you know about that?" Sal cringed.

"I have ears all over this place." Thea shook a finger in his face.

"No. No. She's not one of those," Sal sang. "This woman is a schoolteacher. She's smart. She's compassionate. And she's oh so beautiful."

"She sounds lovely."

"She is," Sal mused. "But I have a problem. Well, I have two problems." He raked his fingers through his hair.

"What's that, sweetie?" Thea set her palms flat on the counter in front of Sal.

"Florence, that's her name, lives near Pittsburgh," Sal explained. "She was here last week visiting the Fair. So, I don't know if I'll ever see her again. I don't even know her last name."

"What else do you know about her? Besides that she's a schoolteacher?" Thea begged the question.

"Not much, but I want to know everything about her." Sal grinned wide, forgetting that he was in a crowded diner. "I can't stop thinking about her."

"Here's what you do," Thea said. "You write her a letter and tell her you want to see her again and you make the trip to see her."

"But I just told you I don't know her last name," Sal replied.

"Then you hope and pray that a letter gets to her," Thea offered. "What's your second problem?"

"I'm seeing another dame. Angelina."

Thea grabbed the small tablet out of her pocket and bashed Sal over the head with it. "Why didn't you tell me that to begin with?"

"Sorry--" Sal raised his hands over his head preparing to block Thea's rage again.

"Does Angelina know about this Florence?" Thea asked.

"Yes, they met last week." Sal lowered his arms in retreat.

"But does she know about your feelings toward Florence?"

"I don't think so," Sal replied. "Angelina is smart enough to think that since Florence was only in town for a few days that she isn't a threat. I like Angelina, but I love Florence."

Thea scratched her head with a pencil. "You need to end things with Angelina before you contact Florence. It's the right thing to do."

"I knew you would say that."

Without warning, Thea swatted Sal over the head with her tablet again.

* * * *

The next day, Sal met Angelina in front of her house.

He held her hand in his, in hopes of soothing her. "Angelina, I think you're real swell. You're cute as a bug's ear."

She gazed at him; her mouth curved upward.

Sal continued, "But I don't think we should go steady anymore."

"Oh." Angelina let go of Sal's hand and dropped hers to her sides.

"You're smart and you'll find a man who loves Greek philosophers as much as you do," Sal explained.

"I thought you liked seeing Robert Frost the other night?" Angelina's eyes swelled, but no tears fell from her face. Sal figured she was too strong to show her pain to him.

"I did," Sal said, "but I don't see us getting married."

Angelina stared down at her feet. "I liked you, Sal." She blew out a long, low sigh.

"I liked you, too, but I don't want to lead you astray." Sal held his breath, unsure what she would say next.

She bit her lower lip and played with her fingers. "Well," she said, her voice cracking, "if that's how you feel, then I guess that's what has to be."

"I'm sorry, Angelina." Sal kissed her forehead and left her on the sidewalk. He didn't dare turn around to see if she started crying. He couldn't feel bad about it, not if he wanted to pursue Florence. Angelina would be fine. She'd continue her love of learning. If she found a husband along the way, then all the better.

When Sal got home, he rummaged through his mother's desk and found a piece of paper and an envelope.

He wrote:

Dear Florence,

It was lovely to meet you last week. I was taken by your beauty and charm. Do not worry, my intentions are pure. I have ended my relationship with Angelina and I am yours if you will have me. I would love to visit you.

Salvatore

After saying a small prayer that the letter would reach her, Sal wrote on the envelope:

Once Upon a Time in Chicago

Miss Florence, a schoolteacher
Jeannette, Pennsylvania

# # #

The End

Author's Notes

Florence received the letter.

The reason I know this is because Sal and Florence are my grandparents.

After several months of letter writing, Sal and Florence met again in late December 1933 when Sal came to Jeannette, Pennsylvania. Two weeks later, they became engaged. Since Florence's family was from central Italy, Bartolomeo and Theresa didn't initially approve because they considered it a mixed relationship. Once they realized how much Sal was in love, they relented. Sal and Florence married on September 3, 1934. They lived and worked in Jeannette and then retired to Venice, Florida. They were married for 59 years until Sal died on November 10, 1993, at the age of 84. Florence lived seven more years and died at 93 on May 25, 2000. They had two daughters, Teresa Mercedes and my mother, Gaetana Adrienne. Sal did most of the cooking!

This book is inspired by a true story of my grandfather's coming of age in Chicago in the early 1930s. Yes, Sal defended his father to a bagman at Bartolomeo's tavern. As a result, a couple of years later, Bartolomeo's tavern was bombed. Sal claimed that he worked for one of Al Capone's lawyers, but I don't know the name of the man. Eddie Devine is fictional. Sal also claimed that Al Capone unexpectedly showed up at a family wedding (Chapter 4), but that was the only encounter with the notorious gangster. And, believe it or not, Capone set up a soup kitchen for the unemployed in Chicago during The Great Depression.

Sal claimed he heard the shots of the St. Valentine's Day Massacre in 1929. But as I researched the time and date, I have to question that. Sal was taking classes at the time at the University of Illinois. The massacre happened on a Thursday morning around 10 a.m. on the north side of the city. Sal lived on the south side of the city, a good ten miles away. If he heard the shots, what was he doing on that side of town at that time of day when he should have been taking classes or at home? I guess I'll never know.

Joe Aiello was a real gangster at the time, but, as far as I know, Sal never encountered him. However, based on my research, Aiello's death is accurate.

All of the newspaper headlines are verbatim from *The Chicago Daily News* and *Chicago Tribune*.

My grandfather was a reformed letch. Before he met Florence, he gambled, he smoked, and he was popular with the dames. He often told the story that he was seeing a married woman and jumped out her second-story window when her husband unexpectedly came home. Mae Russo is based on that woman.

Once Upon a Time in Chicago

Paolo is a fictional character. He is based on Sal's cousin, Sam Scroppo, who owned a trucking company that held the contract to haul freight on the Chicago River docks. My family suspects Sam was thoroughly involved with the mob. My mother received a few gifts from Sam that she believed 'fell off the back of a truck'.

Thea is also fictional. Lou Mitchell's Diner on West Jackson Boulevard is a real iconic diner that's been serving hearty breakfasts and lunches since it opened in 1923. I'm not sure if Sal ever ate there, but it seems like a place he would have gone.

Most of the names of Sal's family members are correct except for Phil's wife and Faye's husband. Phil's wife's real name was Rose and Faye's husband's real name was Salvatore. I changed them to Joyce and Nicholas, respectively, so as not to confuse them with other characters.

The night that Sal met Florence, he was dating a woman who Angelina is based on. He also encountered an old girlfriend at the same time (Sophia is based on her). Talk about awkward!

Special thanks to my friend Jasper Choi for the book title!

Love Letters from Sal to Florence

Sweetheart Darling,   November 22, 1933

Am sorry I couldn't write sooner. First it was a funeral and then a wedding, plus plenty of schoolwork. That's life. It goes on and on…

My mother's "comari" died and our family had to pay respects due a dear friend. That old gang of mine is getting smaller and smaller. My friend Ray got married after a courtship of 10 year duration. How's that for a lasting friendship? My "profs" been giving us our 10 week exams. Now can you understand why I've been neglecting you, or is it neglect when a person doesn't write, but loves like I do?

Honey, why cut up your snapshot like that? Here, I've been trying to figure who was standing alongside of you. I like your picture - my honey is a honey "all ways". Still I'd like to picturize the rest of that snapshot. It's not curiosity, it's plain jealousy!! See how jealous us Italians are(?) Italian man is the most dominant toward his woman kin. Italians want their women all to themselves, and no foolin'. Do you still like me after this bit of expressed observation?

Once Upon a Time in Chicago

Day by day, in every way, I go for you in a bigger way. Our love is real - everlasting is the right word for our love. And when we will have each other, we will love with all our might because of the parted suffering we are going "thru". Even if the Gods decide to keep us apart, my love for you will be the greatest that has been.

Why look out of the classroom window dear and imagine if I really exist - I do! Just keep your chin up and smile... Maybe you are in love!!! Persons in love daydream just like you. Or shall I include myself in the same category - that's what I do too - daydream of you!! Only when I wake up, I know that you are real, even if I've never taken you in my powerful arms and smothered you with kisses!

I do about the same thing too; I tear your letter apart and try to read the hidden passages in some of your sentences. About a week ago, before I was busy, I relaxed and read every letter you sent to me. I have them all - they're priceless to Sal Barth.

And this I know is the one true light,
Kindled to love, without much fight,
And when I love, I love with all my might,
Can't you see - I want your love outright...!!
-Amateur Poet

Read the above poem over and over again. There's something in it I want to put across. Let me know your reactions, will you dear.

Shields Ave must be in the book because I saw it before I sent it. The reason I wrote "Ave" after Archer was to show what "a" stands for; "s" stands for street, etc. Shields might not be on the map because it's a short street. I live near Comiskey Park (Home of the White Sox of the American League). When you were in Chicago, you were just about a mile away from my house. The World's Fair sky ride can be seen from my bedroom.

This isn't the picture I promised you. I misplaced it, but I had my promise to keep so I sent this one. Just as soon as I find the other one, you shall get it. It was taken this summer right after a foursome in golf. Oh yes, I like golf. It's a great game after one learns it!! The scenery on the right and left of me are not much competition, even in golf. Is that what you wanted me to say(?) Believe it or not, but it's the truth. Did you ever hear that song - "You're the one I care for"?

Must I wait until I come to Jeannette before you tell me if you care that way about me. I see my little girl doesn't really know if she loves her man.

It's positive - I will come to Jeannette real soon. One of these days you will get a letter telling you when I'll get there. I may stay a week, or a few days, or I may stay two weeks. I'm not sure how long yet, but I'm really coming to see my heart's desire. Are you happy?

So, your mother thinks I'm perfect!! I'm glad she likes me because the fight will be easier for us with her rooting on our side. My mother likes you too judging from the photograph and what I've told her about you. Our mothers are mutual.

If KDKA is on 98 you can't get WCFL. "For Woman Only" those questions aren't bad. I once had a course in Birth Control and Marriage. We had females in the class; I never saw girls blush so much... Insurance companies ask some personal questions!!

So, I can take it - you do all the talk and I'll keep smiling. What do you talk to me about? Come on honey tell me!! I've got a confession to make - I kiss you now and then too!

You answered soon enough - only keep on doing it and maybe you can teach me to write prompt too.

Yours forever and ever. I love you truly.
Sal Bx

Caro signoro e signora Antonio Cipullo -   February 15, 1934

Questa est una lettera de discutere una affari della massima importanza. Ci quanto onore posso recevere io violio la vostra figlia Xelomenna per la mia sposa. Lo viola bene a Xelomenna , e Xelomenna violia bene a me. Per cio, moi cercoma le vostro permesso di matrimonio.

Cari saluti, me firmo.

Roughly translated to: (Florence's given name was Philomena)

Dear Mr. and Mrs. Antonio Cipullo -

This is a letter to discuss business of the utmost importance. How much honor I can recite I want your daughter Philomena for my bride. He *violates* him well in Philomena, and Philomena wants me as well. For this, I am seeking your approval for marriage.

Best regards, I sign.
Salvatore Scavuzzo

Once Upon a Time in Chicago

Florence my dear: May 13, 1934

Now that exams are over, I'll write a long, long letter. I know that I can't make up for lost time, but there's no harm in trying. You may think that I've been neglecting you - I haven't, darling - my thoughts have been of you constantly. Your Salvatore was a busy man!! In the last two weeks, I studied for and took five exams besides taking care of the ticket sales for the dance. Remember me saying "my work first, you second!" Darling, I practice what I preach. Now you can get revenge by letting me wait two weeks - don't you dare Florence!! If you do, sweetheart, the bible says, "An eye for an eye!" I'll double that - oh, I forgot, this isn't a bridge game....

I know it's hard for you to understand that sometimes, I too break promises. If I promise something, I'll do it, but not on time - except with business matters. Since you worship me like an idol, I should write when I say. But honey, I'm not an idol. Idols are Gods - the perfect being. That's what makes me human! I wouldn't want you to be perfect. Some of your faults make my life interesting. This is only one of the many reasons why I want you for my wife. An illustration why I love you so much - I didn't write for 14 days, still you sent me three letters during that period of time. You don't know how much they helped to weather the storm during exam week. They gave me assurance that you were thinking of me even if I didn't write. Florence, sweetheart, you're one in a million - I knew that when I asked you to be mine.

Another thing that kept me from writing sooner - we moved to better living quarters. Now we live in the first floor front. My sister Faye lives above us. I had to do all the decorating - I can do that too! What color do you want our bedroom done in?

My mother is up and around again! She feels better day by day, but how long will it last? When sickness comes, it's hard to get rid of. Isn't it enough to have my mother sick - now that she is on the road to recovery, our Delores gets sick. The doctor claims she caught a cold, later turning into "flu". She's been in bed for two days now.

My mother thanks you for the beautiful card you sent her for Mother's Day. Our mothers made us ....

If every little thing goes right, I'll be seeing you on Saturday night. I just can't wait until Wednesday, I'll know by then if I can come to Jeannette. Then, if I do come, it's only for a day. Oh well - being with you one day is better than not being with you at all. And we have so much to talk about! Our wedding plans will be the main topic. We will straighten the small details then. I find it difficult to write the many things I want to say, I'd need a ton of paper. Another thing, I can talk way faster than I write.

It's alright with me if you don't want to go to New York on our honeymoon. I think your plan is much better. A few days alone will make us love each other all the more! If we went to NY, we'd spend most of our time visiting the 101 relatives I have there.

No darling, five is the limit. All over that number you will have to explain. Our children can be all Neapolitans for all I care, as long as they grow up honorable like their father and mother. While we're on the subject - what's the matter with the Sicilians? Listen woman, wanna start a fight? Chocolate can't bribe a Sicilian!! Let me ask you one question - can Neapolitans make love like some Sicilians I know can. I know what you're thinking of "My Salvatore is one and I'm proud."

Florence, I love you! Never before have I experienced the love fire that burns in my heart. I sense it throughout the day and at night. I try to think what you are doing every minute. Right now you are sleeping (11 p.m.). Even when I sleep, my dreams are of you. The next morning when I awaken, I start anew.

That's right, six X's stands for sixty in Latin. In the underworld, X marks the spot. In love, X means a kiss. In math and chemistry, X is the unknown quantity. Still they all have the same symbol. Real kisses are the best - there is no substitute for kisses. Candy kisses won't do!!

After I read the poem, the impression I got was that of a mother raising her young. They grow up and leave her. Still she loves them and if they would need her, she would come a 'running.

Not much more to say, it's getting late. Will write again during the later part of the week.

Florence, I love you, I love you, I love you! Now you are sure that I love you....

Sal Bx

Spaghetti a la Scavuzzo with sauce

(Chapter 16)

Ingredients for meatballs:
- 1 pound ground chuck
- ½ pound ground pork
- 1 egg, beaten
- ¼ tsp. minced garlic
- ½ tsp. of each: dried basil, salt, dried parsley, black pepper
- 1 cup Italian breadcrumbs
- 1 tbsp. parmesan cheese

Directions for meatballs:
- Preheat oven to 350 degrees F
- Mix the meat with all ingredients in a large bowl
- Form balls 1¼" (approx. size of a golf ball)
- Arrange meatballs on cookie sheet with 1" sides
- Bake for 20 minutes
- Set oven to Broil
- Put cookie sheet on highest rack in oven
- Broil meatballs for 5 minutes - watch them so they don't

burn

Once Upon a Time in Chicago

Ingredients for sauce:
- 2-3 tbsp. olive oil
- ½ cup chopped onion
- 3 cloves minced garlic
- 1 cup mushrooms (optional)
- 1 tsp. dried oregano and basil
- ¼ tsp. black pepper and salt
- 1 cup water
- 28 oz. can crushed tomatoes <u>OR</u> 10-12 fresh tomatoes with skins removed (approx. 2 pounds)
- 6 oz. tomato paste
- ¼ cup red wine
- 1 tbsp. sugar

Directions for sauce:
- In large pot on medium heat, combine first 6 bullets
- Saute until garlic and onion are light brown (approx. 5 minutes)
- Add meatballs, water, tomatoes, tomato paste, red wine, and sugar
- Turn heat to low and simmer covered for 3 hours

Directions for pasta once sauce is cooked:
- Fill 6 quart pot with water
- Add 3 tbsp. salt to water

- Bring to boil
- Add 1 pound of your favorite pasta
- Cook 1 minute less than instructions on the box
- Drain water
- Add cooked pasta to sauce mixture
- Sprinkle with parmesan cheese

Notes:
- Serves 5-6 people
- If sauce is too thick, add 1-2 tbsp. of water at a time to thin
- If sauce is too thin, add another 6 oz. can of tomato paste
- *Bon Appetit!*
- As Bartolomeo suggested, Sal made this nearly every Sunday for Florence.

Once Upon a Time in Chicago

Once Upon a Time in Chicago

Thank you for reading my book.
If you enjoyed it, won't you please take a moment to leave me a
review at your favorite retailer?
One or two sentences are perfectly fine.
Help an author out. ☺
Thanks!

Want some cool merch from me?
Post a pic of this book on your social media and tag me!
@marywalshwrites

Tag me on:

    **BB** aℕauthor

**Sign up for my sometimes-monthly newsletter and
order autographed books at:**
marywalshwrites.com

Follow me on Goodreads and Amazon:
www.goodreads.com/goodreadscommarywalshwrites
www.amazon.com/author/marywalsh2